Frederick William Robinson

Wrayford's ward and other tales

Frederick William Robinson

Wrayford's ward and other tales

ISBN/EAN: 9783337137106

Printed in Europe, USA, Canada, Australia, Japan

Cover: Foto ©Andreas Hilbeck / pixelio.de

More available books at **www.hansebooks.com**

BY

F. W. ROBINSON,

AUTHOR OF

"GRANDMOTHER'S MONEY,"

&c. &c.

IN THREE VOLUMES.

VOL. III.

LONDON:

HURST AND BLACKETT, PUBLISHERS,

13, GREAT MARLBOROUGH STREET.

1872.

The right of Translation is reserved.

LONDON:
PRINTED BY MACDONALD AND TUGWELL, BLENHEIM HOUSE,
BLENHEIM STREET, OXFORD STREET.

LONDON:
PRINTED BY MACDONALD AND TUGWELL, BLENHEIM HOUSE,
BLENHEIM STREET, OXFORD STREET.

RICHARD ARNOTT'S CRAZE.

(CONTINUED.)

CHAPTER III.

REVELATIONS.

I DID not sink from the editorship of a Magazine to the old occupation of reviewer—I sank to abject poverty. It was with the greatest difficulty that I could dispose of an article; the places that I could have occupied were filled. I had made many enemies, and no friends. I dragged on existence for two years, passing from one office to another, writing for cheap publications (the cheap publications of forty years ago!) and where the pay bestowed upon me just kept me from the workhouse. I was destined for another change, perhaps the greatest.

Amongst some hundreds of advertisements which I answered in my time, was one for a secretary and amanuensis. I replied in a listless way, and not dreaming of success —success which had been engulphed in the blackness of despair long since ; but to my astonishment I received a letter asking no questions concerning me, but accepting my services without a word of explanation. Could it be a trick—a cruel jest to betray me into a useless journey to Westmoreland ? It seemed strange that without a word as to my character or ability, I was accepted by one to whom I must be an entire stranger. It was impossible that my name could have been recognized, even as editor of the magazine which I had conducted it had been kept a secret, and my letter had been laconically couched, and had no merit in its composition. Still I resolved to hazard the journey. I felt it was a risk ; that it involved more than my pecuniary means could afford; yet I bargained away the last of my favourite books, as I had bargained away so many before, and started on my journey.

*　　*　　*　　*　　*　　*

When I stood before Hartford House, near Kendal, Westmoreland, I believed myself to be the dupe of some inconsiderate idiot. It was a large mansion of dark red brick, half overgrown with ivy—an Elizabethan edifice of imposing exterior.

Whilst I stood at the gate, the object of the keenest scrutiny to the old lodge-keeper and his wife, a carriage came quickly along the road, wheeled round, passed me, and stopped before the house.

"Do you want anything, young man?" asked the old lady from the lodge-window.

She had lost all patience, and had opened the casement to make full inquiry.

"Is this Mr. Walton's mansion?"

"Yes;" with a disparaging look at my consumptive portmanteau.

"Thank you.   I shall find Mr. Walton at home, I suppose?"

"He has just come in," she replied; "but if you've got anything to sell——"

I walked on rapidly. I knocked at the door, and a footman in dark livery responded to the summons.

"Is Mr. Walton within?" was my first inquiry.

"Yes, sir."

"Can I see him?"

He looked at me critically, and murmured,

"Yes, I suppose so.   What name?"

"Arnott."

I stepped into the hall, and waited on the marble-chequered pavement for the return of the domestic.

I could hear my own heart beating with suspense, keeping double time to the old-fashioned hall-clock ticking a few paces from me.

In less than two minutes, which might

have been two hours counted by my tension of nerve, the servant returned. His late supercilious manner was replaced by a respectful demeanour.

"Will you step this way, if you please, sir?"

I followed him into an adjacent room, where he announced "Mr. Arnott." A pale-faced elderly gentleman, with long grey hair that touched his shoulders, rose with difficulty as I entered.

"I have as much pleasure in welcoming Mr. Arnott," he said, "as I have in the knowledge of my new auxiliary's ability."

"I am honoured by the confidence that you seem to place in me," I observed, "although I cannot understand how I have deserved it."

"That you will know presently," he said, with a smile at the puzzled expression of my countenance.

To say that my heart bounded towards my benefactor—what was he else?—would be only to half express the warm feeling it seemed thrilling with. I had grown very poor; I had known so little sunshine; I had been so deplorably unlucky!

At dinner there was a fresh surprise for me, in the entrance of a young lady of two or three and twenty years of age, tall, graceful, and beautiful—yes, very beautiful.

She acknowledged my introduction with that ease which had characterised her father's reception of me. There was that manner with both father and daughter that is more difficult to catch than half the sciences, the way to please and set at ease all in contact with them.

A few hours later in the evening, a gentleman entered the room with the careless freedom of a friend sure of his welcome; he was introduced to me by the name of Tresanda. He was a remarkably tall man, topping by some inches Mr. Walton; his features were dark and swarthy, and in his large, black eyes, there was little repose and less tenderness. He was particularly courteous in his manner towards me, conversed freely on the passing events of the time at home and abroad, and showed a well cultivated mind, some knowledge of men and men's motives, a lively fancy and a brilliant wit, which would have made him with most persons an agreeable acquaintance.

Despite all these qualifications, there was something antagonistic in me towards him that I endeavoured to shake off—a repellent quality which led me to imagine that he was conversing urbanely with me, and yet laughing at me slyly meanwhile —weighing beneath his polite attention every word that I uttered. I did not like the eyes, there was an unsteady light—a wavering, glittering light in them —that seemed false, and I believe—writing this many years afterwards, and taking into account all that happened between us in that cruel past—that the antipathy which

I had conceived for this stranger was not without its counterpart in him.

I observed, too, in the daughter Olivia, a slight shrinking from the attention which he paid to her, a perceptible shade of dislike, or perhaps of coquettish indifference. They were evidently betrothed; I had formed that surmise before he had been in the room five minutes, and I imagined that some little quarrel had taken place at a former period, which she seemed now inclined to resent.

After Mr. Tresanda had departed, which was at an early hour, Mr. Walton said, " If my daughter will excuse us, you and I will adjourn to the study, Mr. Arnott. I wish to put you on duty early to-morrow morning. I will point out your first task this evening, if you will allow me."

" A task which I shall commence with pleasure," I replied.

He led the way to a small room, at one end of which was a large bay window opening on the garden. He drew the blind up and revealed the spacious grounds, white and silvery in the moonlight.

" You have a fair landscape of garden ground," I remarked, as I stood before the window looking out.

" You should see it in the sunlight," he said, as he looked for some papers in his desk; "then it is at its best. I believe, but for that garden, I should never have written some of my stories. One turn round it, when my mind is hard pressed, brings me a score of ideas. Oh! here is the MS."

He drew some papers from the desk, and laid them on the table. At the same time I uttered an ejaculation of surprise which startled him.

" What is the matter? Do you observe anything?" he cried, joining me at the window.

" Do you see in the deep shadow by the wall? There—something is moving."

" My dear sir, your long journey has made

you nervous," he said, with a laugh ; " what object could anyone have standing in that unenviable position ? Why, the nights grow frosty, and the peaches are gathered !"

I left the window at his request.

"There is my first commission," said he, handing me the papers. "I wish them copied with all despatch.   Let me see if you can read them.   My hand shakes terribly, and I can scarcely decipher my own manuscripts now ; I suppose I am getting beyond work, although I don't like to own that."

Accustomed to the perusal of manuscript, I made out with little difficulty the first few lines.

"That's well," said he ; " you will be of service to me.   And now, Mr. Arnott, a solemn promise."

"It must be an extraordinary request with which I cannot comply."

"I have a peculiar fancy of my own," he said ; " a secret, if you like the word better, which is known only to my daughter, and which I must entrust to you.   Are you to be trusted ?"

"I hope so."

"Laconic," he said, "but I object to florid protestations.   The promise I require is, never to speak of my writings, or allude to me as their author.   I am in love with the anonymous.   It's a craze perhaps—but then everyone has a craze !"

"Ah ! that's true."

"I might have made an amanuensis of my daughter," he said; "but I had not the heart.   When I received your letter amongst two hundred others—two hundred able men shrieking for employment, whilst two hundred thousand fools mismanage business in every shape and form !—when I received your letter, I remembered a service which you did me some years since, and accepted you at once."

"A service of mine ?" I exclaimed. "There must be a mistake."

"Oh ! no," smiling at my astonishment;

"do you remember reviewing 'Etherby,' in the —— paper? That review lost you your berth."

"You—you are the author of 'Ether-by?'"

He bowed, and laughed at my surprise.

" And how—how came you to know— ?" I began.

"Easily enough," he interrupted. "My publisher had dropped hints of a probable attack on my work in the journal on which you were engaged. The proprietor was his bitter enemy. I looked for the article with some anxiety, I must confess. Imagine my astonishment! I heard the true story a year afterwards, and made a note of your name, wondering if I should ever hear of it again, or be of service to you. I am glad to have an opportunity of making this poor return, although I am sorry for your own sake that it is necessary."

I could not speak; my heart was too full. I did not know whether it was joy, sorrow, pride, or shame, that mastered me as I stood there dumb and trembling.

"We will change the subject," he said kindly; "now for my instructions."

After a few minutes further conversation, we returned to the parlour.

"Olivia," said he to his daughter, as we entered, "I have made my new friend our confidant."

"May I thank him now for his chivalrous defence of 'Etherby,'" she replied, with a bright smile.

"We had better drop 'Etherby' for the nonce," said Mr. Walton. "Do you know, Mr. Arnott," turning to me, "my daughter has had her literary ambitions, and used to write once in a mysterious fashion, and bewilder her elders and herself. Crazy too, you see?"

"I gave up my ambition years ago," said she.

"So much the better," answered her father; "why should you grow prematurely old in failing to please the libraries, Avilio!"

"Avilio!" I exclaimed.

Both father and daughter regarded me with surprise.

"Your pardon," I stammered forth; "but —but—I—I have seen that name appended to magazine articles, which I have read and —and admired."

"Thank you, Mr. Arnott," said Olivia. "You are my only admirer. I killed the Magazine, and the editor too. It was a just retribution for his printing my girlish follies!"

I felt my cheeks reddening.

How little did they think of Olivia Walton's MSS. lying in my portmanteau, resting beneath the roof from which they were sent forth! How happy I felt that night! I was dwelling in the same house with Avilio. Why did it never strike me that Avilio was the anagram of Olivia? I pressed the papers to my lips in reverence that night. I had seen the author, and she was young and beautiful, as I had conjectured in the wild fancy of the Past; and I—what was I? One sundered from her; a dependent, a man that had had only one dream in a plodding, thankless life, and that had faded with the morning!

Yes, it was a great craze!

CHAPTER IV.

THE WATCHER.

I ENTERED into the routine of my duties with a resolution to please my employer by concentrating my whole energy to his service. I found him a generous, warm-hearted patron and friend, but I was as far from happiness as ever, though I saw Olivia every day.

Heaven be witness how I loved that girl! What was the passion born of romance in the dark London office, where my magazine was published, to this new devotion, unseen and fierce, that was eating into the very core of my heart?

And Tresanda—with his giant form, his dusky features, and his fiery eyes—was he not the spirit of evil hovering over the woman I idolized?

There was a mystery about Olivia. They were engaged, but she did not love him, I was assured—her whole manner was as that of one resigned to an inevitable fate; he knew it as surely as I did.

Tresanda did not improve upon further acquaintance. The politeness which, out of respect to Mr. Walton, he had assumed at our first meeting, was quickly set aside for a supercilious indifference to my presence. With all his knowledge—for he was a clever man—he was one of those little-minded beings who are jealous of the merest trifles. I have seen him bite his lips savagely when Miss Walton, unconscious of offence, had turned from him to exchange a few words with me.

And yet, that sensitive girl, whose heart

a word less gentle than usual could wound, was to become that sullen being's wife.

Time passed on. I had been in Westmoreland six months; I had spent Christmas beneath the roof of Hartford House, when I met with a singular adventure. One night, in the early Spring, I again observed the shadowy figure lurking by the garden-wall—I had forgotten what had occurred on the first night in my new abode, till a repetition of the incident brought it to my recollection. It was a moonlight night such as the figure had chosen before for its watch; and there, in the same position, at the same place, was the black, indistinct outline of a man, motionless and statue-like. With what object could any one be waiting there? Did it bode evil to my patron's house? I resolved to confront the intruder.

I extinguished my light, and crept cautiously down the stairs; I unfastened the door leading to the garden, and went on stealthi-

ly in the shadow of the wall, making noiselessly towards the watcher.

When I had reached the tree which I
had chosen for a landmark, I peered
round, and discovered the stranger within a
dozen yards of me. Unconscious of my approach, he was leaning against the wall, with
a fixed stare at the house that I had quitted.
I stepped into the path, and suddenly con-
fronted him. My appearance, as if from
the clouds, only gave him a momentary
surprise, which he instantly recovered from,
to fix a bold, unflinching gaze at me.

"I demand to know what errand you
have in these grounds at this hour of the
night?" I asked sternly.

"Demand!" echoed he, in tones as stern
as my own.

"I have a right to demand it. Who are
you?"

"Who puts so abrupt a question to me?"
he said, substituting a second interrogative in
lieu of a reply.

"You must have evil ends to answer in lurking here," I cried—"no right constitutes you a spy and watcher of this house. I have seen you in this spot before, and you must be a stronger man than I, if you leave it without an explanation of your conduct."

He hesitated, then said suddenly—

"My name is Peverton. It will save a scene to tell you this, perhaps. All other explanations I refuse; and now, if you would save your friends within from trouble, do not speak of my intrusion at this hour. I had hoped to go away in peace and silence, harming no one."

"Peverton!"

We were in the moonlight now—the hat which had fallen back from his face revealed features which I had not forgotten. "Mark Peverton!" I whispered.

Yes, it was my school-boy friend—the long-lost face I had not thought of seeing again. He had changed; the face was thin, the eyes sunken, but the expression was identical with that which had stamped his boyish features with so winning a grace at Belton House.

"You have the advantage of me," he said coldly.

"Mark Peverton, I can believe that no unworthy motive prompts your mysterious conduct. You remember Richard Arnott?"

"Is it possible?" he exclaimed. "You Arnott!"

Our hands met with a grasp of iron; we had both suffered, and the past school-time was not wholly forgotten.

"Arnott," he said, after a pause, "meet me to-morrow afternoon at the footpath in the wood. I may explain all to you then. I am bewildered now."

Before I could reply, he had passed to the end of the garden, and had crossed a quickset hedge that divided it from an extensive orchard.

I returned to the house, and spent the night in thinking of him.

On the following afternoon I waited for Mark Peverton in the wood. A few minutes after my own arrival, he advanced towards me.

"You are punctual, Arnott," said he, "there is some of the old nature left— you were never half a minute behind time, in the old school-days. Now tell me your history."

He took my arm, and we strode up and down the velvety grass, with the budding branches overhead.

My story did not take long to relate; and when I had finished he began his with a reluctance that wore off as he proceeded.

He had travelled with his mother on the Continent until within the last two years, when they had returned to England, and settled down in the fair county of Westmoreland.

The rest let him tell in his own words:

"Meeting *her*—I speak of Olivia Walton, Arnott—so often at my mother's house, or at her own—thrown into companionship with a young, beautiful, and intellectual girl —you may guess the result. I loved her with all the passion of my nature! At this time the son of an old friend of Mrs. Walton's settled in Westmoreland——"

"Tresanda?"

"That is the name," he said. "This Spaniard, or half Spaniard, had not visited Hartford House many times before he was fascinated by Olivia. It is needless to say that I became jealous of his attentions, and that Olivia shunned them in every way that she could. Emboldened by my fear of losing her, I confessed my love, and wrung from her an acknowledgment that her heart was not indifferent to me. Oh! Arnott, you cannot imagine how happy I felt that night—you cannot conceive one hundredth portion of that happiness."

"Yes, yes, I can!" I answered, huskily; "go on, Mark."

"That happiness was only to be contrasted by the sudden and awful misery which followed. The next day I rode over to Hartford House, for the purpose of making formal proposals for Olivia's hand. I discovered the place in confusion, Mr. Walton and his daughter were in deep distress, and Mrs. Walton lay on a bed of sickness, from which she was never to arise. There was no hope held out to her from the first moment of her sudden illness. I could not speak of my suit at such a time; I returned home with my passion undivulged. Mrs. Walton lingered a few days, and died one Sunday evening. On that night, an hour before her death," he said in an agitated voice, "she spoke of her last wish—a wish formed when Olivia and Tresanda were children—that they should marry two years after her decease. So fixed had been that project in her mind

—she had clung to it with such tenacity, un-mindful of the diversity of disposition and pursuits between them—that nothing could shake her from her purpose. Tresanda had already been accepted by the parents, and now at that hour was my poor girl called upon to make a solemn promise, so that her mother might leave the world in peace. Conjecture the feelings of Olivia, to decide between her faith to me, backed by her own love, and that of a promise to a dying mother—that mother she should never see again! What followed? In hurried words Olivia confessed all that had passed between us—it availed nothing. It had not been confirmed by the parents' consent, and on that consent had rested Olivia's accept-ance of my hand. The mother prayed Olivia to accept this Tresanda—her father, carried away by the feelings of the moment, urged her to acquiesce. The solemnity of the scene, combined with her mother's agony of suspense and entreaty, prevailed—the promise was made, and my whole life became blank!"

In Mark's excitement at the recital of the scene, I had great difficulty in comprehending his statement, he spoke so wildly and incoherently; but it appeared that Olivia had written to him, explaining all that had occurred, and urging him to forget her—imploring him to spare her further pain and visit not Hartford House again, to forget her as though she had never lived.

"As though she had never lived!" he cried, bitterly, " or I had not been born, or the world had never been made! To spare her, I have not spoken to her from that date. We have passed each other in the country lanes and in the village streets with the cold bows of chance acquaintances; but there is that in my heart still that keeps me hopeful. Arnott," he continued, "I have tried to tear myself away from Westmoreland—from all these familiar spots which wound me by their associations with the lost —but I cannot do it. I must haunt the place, like a ghost."

" But have you never spoken to Tresanda, never reasoned with him ?"

" Reasoned !" he echoed. " The man is without reason ! Did he know Olivia hated him beyond any living thing, he would take a selfish joy in marrying her."

" Has she not spoken to him ?" I asked. " Does not her father see the sacrifice that she will be ?"

" Tresanda is clever—he sees only that," was the bitter answer.

It was nearly sunset when we parted from each other. I could afford no consolation to such a case as his. I pitied him, but I was jealous of him too.

About a week after the interview with my schoolfellow Peverton, a great blow fell upon the house in which I was an inmate.

My loved employer—ever gentle and considerate to me—died without a moment's warning, sitting in the chair at his desk, pen in hand, with the unwritten page before him.

CHAPTER V.

THE NIGHT!

MY duties were fulfilled, my task accomplished; I had nothing left me but to go—to leave Westmoreland—to part from Olivia for ever! It was three months since the death of Mr. Walton. I had spent that time in arranging his last work for publication. Olivia was at a friend's house in the neighbourhood; she had been there since the funeral. I had not seen her all those long, dreary months—there had been no faces but the servants to meet mine—the house was full of echoes.

I wrote to Miss Walton, informing her of the completion of my task, and of my intended departure; and on the following morning she arrived, accompanied by an elderly lady at whose house she had been staying. She was very pale, and, in contrast with the deep mourning of her dress, her features seemed cut in marble. But she was very beautiful. As she extended her hand, she said, mournfully—

"I am sorry, dear Mr. Arnott, that another friend, to whom I am deeply indebted, takes so soon a long farewell of me."

Then followed an embarrassing silence, which she broke by asking whether I had fixed the day of my departure.

"I have chosen an early date—next Saturday."

"So soon!"

"I have no right to a further extension of time—it is best to get away."

She inclined her head, as if in acquiescence, and, followed by her friend, she entered the old drawing-room.

I saw the dreamy look which she gave round the room—at her birds, which I had tended during her absence—at the books which *he* had written, and the books of his favourite authors on the table—at the arm-chair in the well-known place—at his likeness smiling at her from the gilded frame as he would never smile again!

I saw her sink upon her knees and weep; I closed the door and went into the lane, shading my own quivering eyelids from the servants as they passed me. I should see her again, thank God!

I met Mark Peverton in the green lanes. It was a welcome meeting, and saved me a journey to his mother's house.

It was a hard parting with this faithful friend, whose interest in my future led him to offer me his services to procure me some occupation congenial to my tastes. He had the power, but gratefully and firmly I declined all help. I had learned to struggle for myself so long, that the offer of even this friend came harshly to me.

"If I fail, it will be time enough, dear Mark," I said, wringing his hand; "not now."

He asked many questions concerning Olivia—how she was looking, whether she was well, if Tresanda had seen her since her father's death, and a hundred eager inquiries, which I answered to the best of my ability; and then we parted sorrowfully. As I turned towards Hartford House, he said—

"This is a last farewell, Arnott. It appears as if it were impossible that we should meet again."

"God speed you!"

We parted, and Mark Peverton's prophecy was a true one—we never met again.

I found Tresanda a visitor at the house on my return, and Olivia lingering there still, as though she had been waiting for him. He acknowledged my presence with a cold bow, and then turned to her, as if converse with me were unnecessary. My heart was too full to feel stung by his coolness, and I received it with an apathy which astonished myself. But I was fired to a frenzy ere he had quitted the house. Having occasion to collect the papers of my late patron before I departed, I withdrew from the sitting-room for that purpose. As I returned, the sound of a deep sob, wrung as it were by despair or intense suffering, startled me, and led me to hasten to the room.

As I reached the door, I heard the voice of Olivia exclaim—

" Another time—speak of this marriage another time. Have some respect for my recent loss, sir."

" I urge you for your own sake as well as mine," I heard Tresanda's deep voice reply. " Why for a mere idle form of reverence, nothing in itself, should we live apart any longer."

"You are unfeeling—cruel!" sobbed Olivia.

I felt the blood flowing more quickly within my veins. I did not know whether to return or to enter and put an end to a conversation so distressing to the woman. Olivia's friend was not there to protect her. Yes, I would enter.

"Shed tears for follies, Olivia," said he; "but not at good advice. Were your mother living, she would intercede for me. By the promise to that mother, I still urge you."

I knew that my presence would be hailed as a release by Olivia; I turned the handle of the door and entered.

Tresanda faced me with a savage scowl.

"Why did you not knock? Why did you come in?" he asked, peremptorily. "Will you never know your place in this house?"

"Presently, sir, I shall."

I sat down, trembling with passion; my hands shook so violently that I could scarcely turn the leaves of the book that, with an affectation of composure, I took from the table.

Mrs. Edwins, Olivia's friend, shortly afterwards entered, and relieved the silence that had fallen upon us all.

"Will you never know your place?" How the words rang in my brain! His insolent taunt at my dependent yet honourable position in the family made me grind my teeth together. Yet for all this, for Olivia's sake, I had formed a resolution to brave his scorn again, and intercede for her —for Peverton. It was a foolish resolution, but I was romantic and vain.

Watching my opportunity, I left the house, to take up my position about half a mile down the road that I knew Tresanda must presently come. I had not long to wait. Cigar in mouth, he came striding down the road. As he advanced, I met him. My passion had abated, and my calmness had returned to me.

"A few minutes' conversation with you, Mr. Tresanda."

"A challenge, Mr. Arnott, eh?" said he, coolly.

I kept step with him, and walked on by his side.

"I have not come in anger, Mr. Tresanda," I said earnestly; "but as one deeply interested in Olivia Walton. I wish you to reflect on your position in reference to that girl—to ask yourself dispassionately whether to sacrifice the happiness of her life be just and manly?"

"Are you a madman or fool? What right have you to interfere?"

"It is a *mad* chance, but then no one will speak. Supposing that she loved another, would you resign her, and fill her heart with gratitude?"

"No."

"Supposing——"

"There, there; good evening," he said. "If it be any consolation to you, my officious friend, I have already heard something like this—a trifle more ambiguously expressed—from Miss Walton herself, and have responded, 'You are pledged to me—I will not release you!' Now go."

He thrust me forcibly back with his hand. My composure, which had been rapidly dying out, wholly left me at this last insult. I sprang at him, and struck him in the face.

"I told you that I should know my place presently!" I cried.

"I will shoot you like a dog!" he shouted furiously. "Name your place and time, if you dare to meet me. Our difference of position shall not balk me of my revenge. Do you Englishmen ever fight?"

I felt a savage kind of joy that it had come to this—this man I hated with all the strong intensity of my nature.

"Yes," I cried, "I will meet you. Where?"

"On Saturday, in the wood. There is

an elm-tree blasted by last Summer's lightning. Do you know it?"

"Yes. The time?"

"Five in the morning."

"Five, then."

He raised his hat with mock politeness, and walked away.

When I was alone in my room at Hartford House, I endeavoured to reflect on all that had passed, but it was useless. Everything was in confusion—my brain ached with its weight of thought, and I reeled about the room like a drunken man, grasping at the furniture for support. I tried to think that I had done right—that Tresanda's death would pave the way for Peverton—that my death, which was the more probable event of the two, would be preferable to a life of toil—to the utter void which absence from the home I was about to quit would create. Think of it in any other light I could not—in its moral light, its rebellion against God's laws, I could not even dwell upon it for an instant.

Feverish and excited, I spent the following day in rambling about the town, and it was not till late at night that I sat in the study, packing my portmanteau. My papers were upon the table, the treasured manuscripts of Avilio amongst them, when the door opened, and, to my surprise, Olivia Walton came into the room.

"You have come back!"

"For an instant. I understand you leave very early to-morrow morning, Mr. Arnott."

"Yes, Miss Walton. But I had intended to call upon you to-morrow to say farewell."

"I thought that you would not go without a word."

"God forbid!"

"May I inquire your intentions as to the future, Mr. Arnott?"

"I have none."

"Will you allow me to exert my little interest in your behalf? I think that——"

"Spare me," I implored. "Thank you for all kind offers; but I have a friend whose interest, if required, will be sufficient for my advancement."

"Then I have only to say ' Good-bye,' to thank you for that little kindness and service to my poor father which you have shown so often, and to leave you.   Good-bye."

As she extended her hand, her gaze fell upon the manuscripts on the table; she paused, and a new look of amazement stole across her face.

" Pardon—forgive me !" I cried, seeing her anxious look of inquiry. "They are my own—my right.   Leave me with them. I have treasured them so long—have garnered them so miserly.   I cannot, *will* not, give them back !"

The red blush suffused her features—I saw that the great craze of my life had suggested itself to her for the first time.   A saddening look deepened on her face, and mingled with the scarlet that was there already; she turned away slowly, bade me "Good-bye" in a voice that was very tremulous, and closed the door upon me.

" *Gone—gone—Avilio !* "

In the early morning I met Tresanda in the wood. I was alone. Hartford House was in the distance—for ever in the distance.

There were two gentlemen with him. The elder of the two advanced to me.

"Where is your friend?"—with a look of surprise.

"My friends are in their graves, sir," I said, in a hollow voice. "I come alone—it is my own choice—I shall be perfectly content."

"But, sir, it is contrary to all rule and precedent," he replied warmly ; "and if—"

"Let him have his own way," interrupted Tresanda ; "he would have it look like murder, perhaps. Lawrence, will you be this man's second?"

"My dear sir, I—" his friend began.

"Oblige me, please," he said emphatically.

The surgeon crossed to me at his command, muttering, "It is a strange business altogether!"

The ground was measured, our places assigned. I stood face to face with my deadly foe—this cool, calculating schemer, who had played his cards so well.

" Are you ready?" asked my second.

" One moment. If I fall, will you fulfil one request? It is a small one."

"Name it, Mr. Arnott."

" In my portmanteau at Hartford House you will find a packet of manuscripts. May I rely upon your placing it in Miss Walton's hands?"

" You may."

"Thank you. Now I am ready."

Slowly the preliminary words were given; the gleaming barrels of our pistols were pointed at each other's breasts.

" Fire !"

Clear and loud rang the reports. I felt myself struck in the left shoulder, and reeled backwards a few paces.

But Tresanda was lying dead in the long grass. I had shot him through the brain.

*　　*　　*　　*　　*　　*

It is finished. With the curse of God upon me, I work out my outcast life alone, uncared for in my exile.

They are married—of my first friend and of my silent love, I know only that.

Do they ever in their happiness of home remember Richard Arnott's history?

WILLIAM SMUDGE'S AMENDMENT.

WILLIAM SMUDGE'S AMENDMENT.

TELL you how it all came about, sir?
Well, I've no particular objection, if
you'll tidy up my conwersation a bit here
and there, and don't put all my ignorance
down of a lump in print for people to have
the larf of me. Make it a bit smooth, sir,
and it's a story that ain't so bad a one—a
reg'lar little love-story, in fact—that came
about in one of the strangest ways, which
has left me wondering ever since at the turn
things take at times.

You'll stare very much to hear that I belonged to the Fancy once, sir; setting in this
out-of-the-way part of Australy, taking pot-

luck with one who has a farm, a wife, and children of his own, and is glad to rest you on your journey for a day or two whilst this wet weather lasts, I daresay, big as I am, you can't imagine it. But I was, sir. I took to the Fancy young, directly my father and mother died a'most, and I went at it with a will, being Nottinghamshire born, and afore I was two-and-twenty years of age I was in a decentish kind of way of doing well. I wasn't one of the light weights, as you may imagine p'raps, but was allers backed to fight my own weight—which was rather difficult to get—barring the noted fellers who went in for belts, and lumps of money, and big print in sporting papers. I don't say that I wasn't a bit ambitious, and that I didn't look for'ard to the time when I should werry much astonish everybody, and be the reg'lar tip-top of the perfesshun. I built upon it, being a hambitious card, though I didn't say a great deal to my pals, for fear of being chaffed too much. But I was getting on slowly and by degrees, had quite gone in for the bis'ness, and given up barge and canal work as a low and wulgar trade, and was always to be heerd on at the "Double Fist" tap, Little Choke Street, Nottingham—which is at the back of what they call the Shambles, where the butchers live, as you may recollect. Well, sir, I was two-and-twenty years of age, six foot two in height, and weighed fifteen stone easy— quite in my prime, I may say—when it came into my backers' heads to match me for fifty suverins a side aginst Leary Sam, who had just come off with flying colours in a mill with Jack Owen of London.

I may say that then I was what the world calls a opiniated man, and, as I hadn't been licked easy, and had won most fights of late days, I felt as sure in my 'art of smashing Leary Sam to fiddle-strings as though the thing was done. Leary Sam was of a different opinion, and in answer to my challenge said, contemptious, that he wondered at my imperence, and at my backers' imperence, in a-challenging of him afore I was known in any way to be desarving of the honour, but that for all that he was *on*, and the first deposit of ten punds must be paid down with his own on Saturday night next at the " Double Fist," afore he should consider the thing settled, or I meant anything but bounce.

All this style of thing, I may say, nat'rally riled me ; it wasn't genelman-like, it wasn't exactly my way of doing bis'ness. I felt that p'raps I had challenged too notorious a karacter, and too tough a customer, but he had no cause to treat me lofty, and it cut me to the quick to have to meet this harrogance in the beginning like of my per-feshunal career.

Well, sir, the money was paid down by degrees, the day was fixed, a sporting genel-man from London came, at our expense, to take notes of the fight, and be umpire and referee, and away we went in a special train one early morning to Cooker's Ground, which is thirty miles from Nottingham, and a wild, rough place it was, where the perlice was not likely to trouble us, but to let us fight it out unto our 'arts' content. I should say that there were eight hunderd people went with us that morning, for we'd made a fuss about the fight, and it was gen'rally known that we were both game uns, who'd afford a pretty sight to our backers for the next three hours arter we'd gone at it. I felt that this was a spectucle, and that the eye of the world was on me; and when the train stopped, and we all clambered up the embankment, and I was met at the top with three loud cheers, and lots of shaking hands, I thought that I should bust with wanity.

Leary Sam was in the same train; we had met on the platform, but he was still full of the haughty dodge, and I wasn't inclined to be werry humble, considerin' the way in which he had treated me. He was a big feller, I saw, who'd take a lot of knocking

about afore the job was polished off, and I
thought that he rather seemed to think the
same of me, for all his marked coolness to
our party.

Now, I daresay you are aware, sir, that
the members of the prize-ring, and especially those genelmen born and bred in Nottingham, are roughish in their ways, and
don't study other people's feelin's a great
deal. They never did in my day, and I've
no doubt it's the same as ever; and I must
say this, that of all the roughest lot of men
ever lumped together in one spot, this was
the werry wust, and I don't know, at that
time, whether I was much better than the
wust of them, though shamed I am to think
so now. P'raps I didn't swear quite so easy
as they did, or drink so much at most times,
or was gen'rally so quarrelsome that I must
make quarrels and fights with smaller people
than myself for the luxury of smashing 'em,
but I was a bad un, sir, and that's the long
and short of it.

Cooker's Ground is a wild bit of country, as I have said, and, indeed, I don't believe there was more than one house—and that a little thatched cottage perched on the side of a road that went over the hills and far away, as the poet says—within five miles of the place. It was exactly the spot for bis'-ness of our description, and he was a gen'us who had hit upon it.

It was an unlucky job, to begin with, that that 'ere cottage should have been right in our line of march to a flat bit of heath a hundred yards ahead and a-top of the fust hill, for the company was in excellent sperits, and not too partikler about the fun they had afore we got to the bis'ness of the day. I guessed that there'd be something on at the cottage as we passed it, that some playful feller would shy a stone in through the latticed winder, or smash the palings down, or let out the pigs, which were grunting at us from a crazy sty in the garden, or make a clean sweep of all the apples that were growing about the place, or hinterfere with the bees which were making honey all the day, after Doctor Watts' receipt, p'raps, or else do somethink silly somewhere. They allers did these things—they allers would wherever they were, with no perlice to look arter them, and I didn't think that pretty little place would 'scape our joking. And, by jingo, sir, it didn't!

I fluster now when I think of those eight hunderd roughs, the werry cream of the back rows and the market, screaming and yelling along till they reached the cottage, where the door was open and three people stand-ing there, open-mouthed with wonder, as well they might be, for sich a sight had never come upon 'em in all the days they'd lived there. There was two old people and one young un—the old uns uncommon-ly ugly even for old uns, and the young un as pretty-faced, rosy-cheeked, and modest a gal as ever was seed, I think, and as ever I had seed, I knew. She stood in the background, peeping over the shoulders of the old people, who must have been the greatest of grandfathers and grandmothers, they looked so extremely ancient by the side of her, and they were so unaccountably yaller. They were full of curiosity, as well they might be, and the old man skreeks out—

"What is it? Is anything wrong with the train? Where are you all going to?—who are you?" and a lot more questions, at which, I am sorry to say, we stood and grinned, and after we had done grinning, we stood and swore, which so scared the three of 'em that they banged the door to and bolted up, as though they were going to bed at once.

If it had ended there, it wouldn't have mattered, and we might have been supposed to behave ourselves as well as might have been expected; but it didn't: it got wus and wus, and some one thought of chairs and tables being handy to stand on for the back rows when the fight was on, and a rush set in which took the front door clean off its hinges, and tumbled a lot of us into the tiled parler, to the fright of those good countryfolks, who went all of a heap into a corner, and began saying their prayers their hardest.

" Oh, dear, you don't want to murder us, please," the old genelman found voice to say at last—" and there's nothing worth your while to steal, I assure you, sirs, in all the place. We're poor, hard-working coun‧try people, and if you won't do us any harm, we'll all be so much obliged to you."

" All right, old bloke," our president said, and having a flow of langwidge, he was entitled to be spokesman for us, and speak he did, at the werry top of his lungs, for everybody was making a row of his own, and it was hard work to be heard. " We on'y want to borrow a few chairs and tables, and anythink to stand upon whilst

the mill goes on—just on the heath a-top
there. Bring 'em all back again, 'pon
honer; shan't hurt anythink—it's a prize
fight, you know."

"Oh, is it?" ejaculated the lady of the
house, coming from the corner as bold
as brass again. "If I didn't think it was
somethink awful by seeing sich a pack of
blackguards trapesing past, and a-hearing of
your wicked words. I won't lend a thing;
and if you touches a thing, I'll have the law
agin' you, mark me, as I'm a blessed woman."

They all larfed at the old lady, and at the
way in which she plucked up a sperit and
shook her fist in the face of the man nighest
to her; but they didn't take much notice of
her sayings, but walked upstairs into the two
top-rooms, and came down with six chairs,
two wash-stands, a stool, and one small chest
of drors, which, added to a deal table and
five more chairs in the parler, made up all
the portable furnitur in stock.

"You wagabones!" cried the lady, "you're never going off with them there things like that ?"

"Hush, grandmother! Oh, pray be quiet, do," said the pretty girl in a whisper, and looking as pale as the ceiling overhead.

"I shan't," answered the old lady, who I must say was like a lioness afore us. "I won't see all my property made off with. I'll not have my place turned out of winder like this, by a parcel of wretches and thieves and the lowest of the low, who ought to know better. Mr. Rasp"—to her husband, who was overtook with palsy, and had shivered his way into the empty fireplace— "if you showed yerself a man, and turned these creatures out, it'd be better for you than standing there, you silly !"

But Mr. Rasp did not see the way to turn us out, and only gave one pitiable look at his wife, and groaned forth—

"Let 'em be, Mrs. Rasp. Don't aggere-wate 'em—pray don't aggerewate 'em."

" We'll bring everythink back," said our spokesman, " if you'll be so kind as to lend us 'em for a few minnits." The first lot were 'arf-way up the hill with the chairs and tables by this time, and a second lot were making free with the tubs and pails they had found in a washus at the back, and which things would come in werry handy, turned bottom uppermost, if they didn't knock the bottoms out fighting for 'em in the front garden. " We won't inconwenience you more than we can help."

" You ought all to be hanged," said Mrs. Rasp, " to come and gut us out like this— you Jack Sheppards and Blueskins—you pack of idle, dirty, thieving rascals. But I'll have the law of yer. I'll go for the milingtery—I'll do somethink."

But the more she scolded the more they larfed, and I larfed with them, until one feller made free enough to creep round and try and kiss that pretty quiet gal, who saw how her grandmother spiled matters by her hinterference, and him I knocked over just as she began to cry for help.

"Stach that, George," I said werry quiet in his ear, when he had picked hisself up agin, and was looking about for a front tooth he missed, " and let the gal be ;" and her look of gratitood for that little attention on my part seemed to make a man of me.

" You'd better be minding your own bis'ness. What right have you to be here? You'd like to see the fight, I dare say, instead of fighting yourself. That'd suit you a great deal better—wouldn't it ? " said George, at last, flying a'most down my throat, and swearing werry much.

"You all clear out of here, you chaps, afore I move a step to the ring," I said. " You've all done harm enuf, without hadding hinsult to hinjury," which was a fine big speech of mine, and rather out of my line, only I suppose I wanted to show off to the gal.

" Thankee, sir," said the old man, and

"Thankee, sir," looked those pretty eyes agin; but the old woman only said—

" You're as bad as any of 'em, you big brute," which was not a kind remark; but then we can't expect, sir, everybody in this world to be grateful for what we do for 'em.

However, they all went out of the house, and I went last, to find about two hunderd of 'em fighting for the pails and tubs still, which were easy things to snatch away from one another, and shy about the garden and at each other's heads. They were losing their tempers fast, and getting more spiteful than playful—taking no notice of the few who shouted for order, and swore because they could not get it—when that old woman of mettle who had sarsed the lot of us, and who in her fits of rage cared no more for her property than we did, stepped out of the back-door with her apron over her head, and with a long clothes-prop tilted over three of her bee-hives in our direction, and then ran indoors agin.

Mussy on us all, I shall never forget that, sir! They came on at us like a harmy, each beastly insect picking out his man, and nailing him to begin with, while a lot more buzzed about us and made bobs at us, and took it in turns to pison us with them dangerous stings of theirn. Well, we ran for it, and some put pails and tubs over their heads, and that made matters wus, for the bees got under and wouldn't come out agin; we went all the way to the ring with the bees arter us, and there the bees stayed the fight out, bobbing about at everybody, and keeping everybody narvous and irritable, doing no end of harm, and making no end of agony.

I am inclined to believe to this werry day that those bees were the cause of my losing the fight, for lose it I did, after forty-three rounds, which took three hours and three-quarters. I think, if it hadn't been for the bees, Leary Sam wouldn't have got the best of it; for he hadn't troubled hisself about the people's furnitur, and his backers had took him straight up to the heath, and kept him cool and quiet, whilst my backers had been worrying the old people and the young un, and I had got mixed up in the matter in the most unnecessawary manner, and got stung three times—once on the nose, once on the chin, and once between the eyebrows. So I started all over sore places to begin with, and when these got dropped on by Leary Sam, it made matters wus by many degrees, and I never knew a nose swell up as mine did. That was my weak point—even when there wasn't a point at all to speak about—and Sam saw that, and made the most of it, till I couldn't see him for nose, and hit out wild and got alto-gether " groggy."

But you don't want to hear of a prize-fight, sir, and the less said about it the bet-ter, now that I've no more to do with the perfesshun, and proud I am to say it, setting

here. It was my dead failure, and I felt
fit to die with rage and martification when
I opened my eyes after a clean floorer,
and was told that I'd been in a swoond for
three minutes, that I wasn't up to time, that
the sponge had been thrown, and that Leary
Sam, with many cheers from his party, had
been named the winner. I fainted away
agin then, and though they said that that
was weakness, I knew better—it was all my
sense of smallness and of being done by
Leary Sam after all his harrogance. I was
told afterwards that Sam stooped down and
shook hands with me afore he went away,
but I didn't see him ; I didn't know anythink
or anybody, and I kep' going off like a
babby direckly they tried to set me on my
feet and walk me down to the station,
which, with the train and everybody else a-
waiting for me, wasn't a nice look-out.
Four of them took me in their arms at last
and carried me until they got frightened by
a medical man—who had paid to see the

fight, and might have known better p'raps—
saying that he thought if they tried to get
me to Nottingham it was jist possible that I
should die. I had tried to do too much,
and so had overdid it, and was altogether
floored, and he wouldn't advise anybody to
take me any furder: all this arguing with
the beastly bees buzzing about still, and
everybody on the look-out, as they had been
all the morning, for 'em, for that Mrs. Rasp
had quite spiled the pleasure of the day,
and made everythink as uncomforable as
possible. However, argufy they must, and
at last they made up their minds to carry
me to the very cottage where we had mis-
behaved ourselves so much, and leave me
there with the doctor for an hour or two,
till I was strong enough to be fetched by a
down train, which they would arrange
should stop for me. The doctor didn't like
the job, but he was afeard of the risk of
leaving me, and—ah! I just was bad, sir;
and when I did feel sense enough to think,

I began to think that p'raps it was all up with me, and that it was a rum way of going out of the world—licked clean off it by Leary Sam for fifty punds.

They got me to the cottage, the few who were left, and found the old genelman, who was a neat carpenter in his way, putting a pair of new hinges on his door, and Mrs. Rasp watching the bis'ness and holding the screws for him. That they were surprised to see me was not to be wondered at a great deal, and that they had no end of objections to a prize-fighter being billetted upon 'em for two hours was very nat'ral to expect, 'specially as they had not been treated well, and I was the only article brought back to the cottage, the chairs, tables, wash-stands, pails and tubs, and chests of drors, being left upon the heath in any fashion, a hunderd yards away. But it was a matter of life and death; the doctor was firm, and talked about the law if anythink happened; and my friends did not stay for much reflecshun, but carried me straight into the room to a sofy-bedstead which was there, and which was a mussy hadn't been taken away with the rest of the things, and there laid me, rather too heavy to be lifted off agin.

"I believe that that wretch is a-going to die here," I could hear Mrs. Rasp say; and then a softer voice, all music like, cried out, "Oh, poor fellow, I hope not," which I took as kind, and which was the last I heard, for I went clean off agin, and did not come to for 'arf an hour, when I found myself alone with the doctor, who was dropping brandy down my throat with a tea-spoon.

"How are you, Bill—better?" he said.

"Eh? oh, yes; I'm better now."

"Don't rub your head, don't touch your nose; you'll be all right presently, Smudge."

Which I didn't feel that I should, nor more did he, for he was as white as a ghost, and narvous for me, I'm sure.

"Let's see, where am I?"

He told me that I was in the cottage at Cooker's Ground, and that the 'habitants were fetching home their furnitur by degrees, and grumbling a good deal still.

" Where's Sam ?"

" He's gone back," he said.

" I should like—another round," I said, at which he bust out larfing, and said he was sure that I should do now, if I was only patient. And patient I was till the two hours passed, and better I felt and sensible, but as weak as any cat that ever lived, and about as capable of going down the hill to the railway as of going in that instant for the champion-belt with Bendigo. The good people had got most of their furnitur back by that time, and werry tired they were with fetching it, and sorry I was I couldn't help 'em in any way.

" Oh," said Mrs. Rasp, as she came in, " he's better, then ?"

" Yes, he's a little better," said the doctor.

"And when will he be off?"

"I am sorry to say that it will be as much as his life's worth to disturb him," said the doctor, as grave as any judge; "and that it will be as much as our lives are worth, too, to try and get him away from here."

"I never!" said Mrs. Rasp; and I don't think that she ever did.

"What—what's to be done?" said Mrs. Rasp.

"Why, he must stay here."

"Good gracious!"

"In the morning, as early as possible, I'll come and see him," said the doctor, "and bring a friend to see him. He'll do for to-night there, as he is; and if you have any arrerroot or gruel, with a little brandy in it, it will be about as much as is good for him."

"And pray who's to pay for it all?" said Mrs. Rasp as sharp as a needle, and the doctor didn't feel able to answer her.

"I ain't hard up," I said here; "I've got

a pund or two by me, and there's a great-coat, nearly new, when that's gone, which'll fetch somethink ; and if you can put up with a feller till the morning, I'll take it kindly on you."

Which was a long speech, and made me dizzy, but I could see that it relieved the minds of the old souls a bit, who looked poor enough theirselves, I must say.

" That's werry well," said Mrs. Rasp, " but the damage to the furnitur ?"

" I'll see what can be done about that," said the doctor, " when I get back."

And I believe he did see, and, being a sporting caracter, went round to the Double Fist, where he was well known, and tried to raise a subscription, which no one seemed to see at any price. So these poor Rasps were in trouble enuf, without me sprawling there with my fifteen stone upon the sofy— put to bed by the doctor and Mr. Rasp —taking up all the room, and such a norrible sight about the nose and mouth that the family supped in the washus rather than catch a sight of me over their meals.

For I became a fixtur there—that was the wust on it, or the best on it, according to one's idea of looking at things. The next day I couldn't have moved off that sofy to have saved my life; I was like a log of wood chained down there, and I knew that I was in a badder way than I had fancied last night.

The doctor came, and a friend of the doctor's—which bringing him was proof enuf what he thought of my case—and there they stood over me, talking of my condishun with myself a-staring at 'em; and I must say they didn't study my feelin's much, or thought, p'raps, that I hadn't got any, being on'y a prize-fighter, you see, or fancied that I wasn't well enuf to understand 'em, p'raps, which was a wrong idea of theirn.

"He's been reg'larly pounded by Sam,"

my first doctor said, " and 'pon my word I don't think he'll get over it."

" It'll make things awkward," his friend said; " there'll be a fuss in the papers, and you can't get off as a witness, which looks bad in your line."

" Yes, it does," said the other; and then, he put his hands in his pockets, and thought a precious sight more of his trouble than of mine. At last he turned to me, shook his head, and said—" What a nuisance you are, Bill Smudge!"

" Yes, sir, but I can't help it," I said back to him, and he called out—

" Hollo, you're sensible, Bill, are you? I thought you weren't. How do you feel now?"

" Oh, anyhow, sir; not quite so spry as I did last night, p'raps."

" Ah, p'raps not."

" How's Sam, sir? Not walking about yet, is he, sir, as if he had had so werry much the best of it?"

"Well, he can't show yet, he's been too much mauled."

"Thank gord!" I said, at which both the doctors chuckled, though I couldn't see anything to chuckle at myself; for, of course, it would have been precious hard for Sam to have been about next day crowing at the Double Fist.

"You ought to have beaten him," said the doctor number one, "for I took the odds against you, Bill."

"Ah, I'm sorry; p'raps when I come round I'll have another try, sir."

But I did not come round in a hurry, and you should have seen the faces of those Rasps when they were told that it was impossible to move me.

"This is a pretty mess," I heard Mr. Rasp say, and his wife said that it sarved him right for not showing a proper sperit, though what the shivery old feller could have done under the circumstances is more than I can tell. However, there I was then, and all the money I'd left at home was sent me by a friend, and the great-coat was given up to 'em, and they were more easy in their minds for awhile, though a nuisance I was, and no mistake, and they didn't mind saying so to me.

All but Fanny Rasp—who was to me allers Fanny Raspberry—for never was a gal more sweet and nice, minding no trouble, and doing all she could for me, as if I'd been a brother to her, instead of a nasty, low, ugly, wicked prize-fighter, as I heard her grandmother call me once, when Fanny wanted to light the fire and make some beef-tea for me. She was exackly like a sister—never put out a bit by my being there, and doing her best to smoothe over the hard things her grandfather and grandmother said, which somehow hurt my feelings, being weak and poorly p'raps, although what they said wasn't far from truth. When I thought that I was a-going to die—about the third day that was—I nodded my head

to Fanny, and said " Thankee," and
swoonded clean off again just as she yelled
out with fright; but somehow they, or she,
got me out of that swoond, and better I was
by degrees arter it; and she nussed me
through it, and never minded the scolding
which she got for wastin' of her time.

They was continiwally scolding her for
somethink. Once I heerd them bully her
because she was what they called a cum-
brance upon them, and as bad as I was;
and when I saw her crying about that in a
corner near the winder amongst the jerra-
niums and fooshers, I did feel riled, for she
was a gal, sir, who hadn't a mite of crossness
in her, but was altogether different from
anybody I ever knowed.

I had been four and a half days there
when she was crying as I told you. I
was beginning to be able to flop from one
side to another, and my nose, which was
uncommonly in my way still, and turning
yaller and green, was going down a bit.

Mrs. Rasp had gone a-marketing to a village five miles off, and Mr. Rasp was digging in the garden, so she could cry, not minding me much, with comfit to herself.

"What's the matter, Fanny?" I said. I called her Fanny somehow because they did, and p'raps because I didn't know any better. "What are you a-cryin' for?"

"Because I'm an orfun, Mr. Smudge," she answered.

"So am I, but I don't cry about it."

"Oh, are you an orfun too?" she asked, drying her eyes upon her apron werry carefully, for it was about Mrs. Rasp's time for coming back.

"Yes, I am."

I hadn't thought much about it afore, but I certainly was an orfun, and as Fanny was one too, I felt rather proud of it at that time.

"You ain't got no father or mother, then?"

"No, I ain't."

" Wasn't they kind to you when they was alive, like mine ?" she asked.

" Well, not pertikerly."

" Oh, dear ! Not your own father and mother ?" she said ; and I can see her round, blue eyes now, and her little, round, red mouth, turned my way from the winder.

" No, not pertikerly. They was fond of fighting atween theirselves, and when they made it up they whacked me, jist to keep their hands in."

" That's why you took to fighting, then, yourself ?"

" It might have gived me the idea."

" And have you been fighting all your life, Mr. Smudge ?—fighting for a living ?"

" Not quite. I've been at barge-work on the canals, and so on."

" Why don't you go to barge-work agin ?"

" I like fighting best."

" Why ?"

" It's a noble art," I said ; and I had allers

thought so, till she came down upon me almost indignant.

" It's a brutal art," she said, all a-red like in the face. " A lazy, hulking kind of life, that can't do any good to anyone, and only makes a brute of you. Oh, the dreadful lot that came that day into this house !"

" Not respectable, sartinly," I said, after a little reflecshun ; " but they was friends of mine, a many of them."

" Then I won't say anythink aginst them," she answers ; " on'y, what friends !"

" They ain't so dusty. You'll find they'll get up a little benefit for me at the Double Fist—a sparring festiwal, or somethink, and that'll help me on till I come round agin. Would your friends do as much for you ?"

" Oh, Mr. Smudge, I ain't got any," she says ; and then she falls a-crying once more, until I said, with an awful growling voice that didn't seem to belong to me, and that made me fancy it had slipped down lower somehow—

" Yes, you have."

" Where ?" she asks.

" Here," says I.

" Oh, a pretty friend you are !" she says, inclined to smile again.

" I don't s'pose you think much of him," I said, and upon my word you'll hardly believe that I was inclined to bellow, and that I was hurting myself a-trying not to do it; " but here he is allers, and if you ever want his help——"

" I don't suppose I ever shall, Mr. Smudge, but thankee all the same."

I thought awfully about that gal after that, and when the doctor came at last, and said that I was better and should be able to go in a couple of days, I was sorry that I couldn't be taken wus agin, for all that I had had to put up with owing to them Rasps, who was the hardest and selfishest of people.

Well, it came to going away at last, and, not to spin this story out too much, I may as well say that it was going away with all my 'art behind me, for in love with that 'ere gal I was, and a pretty feller to fall in love too, with one eye bunged up still, and my nose, though going down beautifully, more like a Winsur pear in size and colour than any-think else in natur. I thought it wasn't possible to make love in that condishun; I didn't feel that it'd be grateful on me, not to mention that she was such a heap too good for me, that I seemed to sink awful small into myself whenever I spoke to her, and the on'y grounds of hequality on which I could meet her was our orfunage. But still I didn't like to go away and say nuffink, and so on the one chance I got to speak to her, I said—

"Fanny, I'm hoff to-morrow."

"Yes," she said meekly, "so it is. You're sure you're strong enuf?"

"I think so, and if it's on'y to make you glad to have the place as it was afor I came

lumping in amongst you, I should go direckly I could crawl."

"Oh, would you?"

I thought she might have said she wasn't
glad at the last, but she didn't, and so I said
myself—

"And glad you are, I s'pose?"

"I'm glad you're better, Mr. Smudge,"
she said, looking down—oh! so shy, sir!

"But not glad that I'm a-going away?"

"No," she said at last, "for you haven't
been much trouble, and have been patient
with it all."

"Well, lookee here," I bust forth with;
"if I come back agin, werry rich somehow
—the winner of a hunderd pounds in a
grand match, or the holder of the Belt
some day—will you be glad to see me
agin?"

"No, I shan't," she said pertly. "I hate
prize-fighters."

This was mortifying to my self-respex,

but I was dead set on Fanny, and felt that anything in human natur for her was worth trying, and I said—

"If I give it up, Fanny, and never go to the Double Fist agin, but take to work——"

"Real, honest, hard work," she put in here.

"Real, honest, hard work," I repeated, "and can show you that I'm arning money week by week, and putting sumfink by for a rainy day—if my nose goes down properly, and I ain't quite so awful ugly—and if I comes up here, and says, 'Fanny, you ain't sorry to see me again?' now what will you say back?"

She thought this over, and then she looked up 'arf laughin' and 'arf cryin' at me, and my poor bruised face didn't seem to scare her, and she answers—

"Willum"—and I didn't know my own name, given out in that genteel manner— "Willum," she answers, "I'll say I'm glad to see you ; but "—and here she turned all a-fire once more—" oh, don't come, never come, if you're not away from this old life of yourn, and all those drefful friends."

" Fanny, it's a bargin."

I shook hands with her, and the next day I went away, thanking everybody for all that had been done for me, and Fanny Raspberry—I never called her Rasp —watched me from her up-stairs winder all the way down hill.

You look, sir, as if it all ended there, but, bless your soul, it didn't ! This was true love, and none of the nonsense that you gets in books, and which my wife reads to me out here, not being yet a scholard myself, though going in for writin' next Winter, when the nights are long. I went back six months arterwards, in the Winter-time—one Christmas morning it was, with snow upon the ground. I went back when all the flowers were dead in the garden, and the bee-hives, I'm happy to say, were empty, and I lifted up the latch of the door, and stepped in, saying—

"A merry Christmas to all here, let's hope !"

And the Rasps looked at me, and Fanny turned pale, and then blushed and smiled—ah ! such a welcome as I ain't forgot, you may be sure. And Mrs. Rasp snapped at me to begin with, which I expected nat'-rally—

" Why, what have you come back for ?"

And the old man jumps up and says,

" Hollo, there's not another prize-fight on, is there ?"

" To make you a little present, mum," I said to Mrs. Rasp, " for all your goodness when I lay ill here arter the match with Leary Sam ;" and then she smiled too—for the fust time in all her life, p'raps—and hoped that I was better than I was. I said Yes, and told her—looking still at Fanny— that I'd given up prize-fighting, and taken

to a reg'lar bis'ness, and that I was barge-
man to a great contractor's on the canal,
and good for two pund a week for the next
twelve months, being as strong as a horse,
and altogether handy at my work.

I told this to Fanny later in the day—for
I was actiwally asked to stay to dinner there
—told it all over agin, and wound up with
a—

"Well, Fanny ?"

She looked up werry shily still, and much
prettier than ever, and said—

"Well—Willum ?"

And then p'raps we both looked rather
silly for a moment, till I said all of a sudden—

"Will you try and trust me now, my
dear—trust yourself with me for life ?"

She turned round, put her little hands in
mine, and said—

"Yes, I will—there !"

And that's how it came about that I gave
up prize-fighting, sir, married Fanny, turned

that horrid name of Rasp into the more genteeler one of Smudge, came over to Australy, and settled down here in this little farm, with her and the little ones to keep me allers happy. And that's my Fanny, sir, who waited on you, and did the 'oners of the house; and pretty she is still, sir, for all the years that have gone past us both since I took her away from Cooker's Ground.

And though I hates prize-fighting, and looks back at it with horror and disgust, and can't make out how ever I used to like it and to live by it, I often think that it was a lucky thing for me I fought Leary Sam of Nottingham for fifty suverins a side.

BURLES: A BAD BOY.

BURLES: A BAD BOY.

THIRTY years ago I was one of a hundred and twenty boys, who, together with a hundred and twenty girls, formed the Free School for the Children of Decayed London Shopkeepers. It does not matter for what decayed shopkeepers, or by what shopkeepers free from decay and in flourishing condition the school was instituted; there it stood, seven miles from London on a country road, a plain red-brick building, of the workhouse order of architecture, an edifice that at first sight was not calculated to educe any great degree of exhilaration from the progeny of decayed shopkeepers in general.

If that desirable institution had been a Government office " open " to public competition, there could not have been greater difficulty in obtaining an appointment. In the first place, there were more children of decayed shopkeepers than there were red bricks in the building erected for their accommodation; and, in the second place, the vacancies were few and far between, and were filled in again like magic. When a vacancy did occur there set in an awful rush of insolvent fathers and mothers to the governor, the deputy-governor, the directors, the secretary, the secretary's man, the secretary's man's man; to the gentlemen who had votes, and the gentlemen who knew other gentlemen who had considerable influence with somebody else.

My widowed mother had to procure cards printed with my name and age, her own name and age, and my poor father's

name and age thereon ; where my father
had lived, how long he had been in business, and the day of the month on which he
had given up business for ever. She had to
put aside her dress-making and "orders
punctually attended to" for a week, take her
only silk gown and some family relics to the
pawnbroker's at the corner of the street, and
then set out on a long, wearisome, canvassing expedition, which lasted till the day of
nomination. As a matter of course, my
mother failed in her first effort; when there
was another vacancy, the whole tedious
business commenced again, to fail again.
Her cards presently began to have imprinted
on them, "third application," "fourth application," "fifth application," and yet there I
was at my mother's elbow, a big lout of a
boy, eating her out of house and home.
When it got to "eighth application," and
one gentleman with a hundred and fifty
votes suddenly took it into his head to
plump them in my favour, I was returned

by a majority of five over one hundred and ninety-three candidates!

I entered the school, and my mother, after all her perseverance in procuring me admittance, cried fit to break her heart when she left me in the great brick house alone.

Boys of twelve years old quickly accommodate themselves to circumstances, and I was soon at home in my new corduroys and Institution buttons. I found the boys of the Asylum neither better nor worse than other boys; I found the diet bad, the lessons hard, the principal master harder. Mr. Maxon was certainly of the inflexible species : an iron-headed, hard-fisted, strong-featured individual, who was always banging his great hand on the desk and startling the hearts into the mouths of his one hundred and twenty pupils.

Charitable Institutions have generally clever and humane men at the head of the working department. I regret to say that

Mr. Maxon was an exception to the rule. No one liked Mr. Maxon. The boys hated him, made hideous grimaces at him behind his back, fell into shivering-fits when he fixed his grass-green eyes upon them, and muttered anathemas when he went through a series of physical-force performances—which he did every afternoon—with a life-preserver sort of cane. Who put him in authority over one hundred and twenty sons of decayed shopkeepers, there was not a single youth in corduroys and buttons to inform me. Who saw his capabilities for so responsible a position, and was struck with his docility and lamb-like characteristics, was equally a riddle—no one knew anything about him, save that there he was to be seen, heard, and endured, every day from six to six in Winter time, from six to seven in Summer.

Justice compels me to assert that he was an industrious man ; he never flinched from his work—in fact, he was rather partial to work, and to seeing others work, and—ugh !

—he was such an unfeeling, stony-hearted being! We were seldom out of his sight; he took the head of the breakfast table in the early morning, and scowled over one hundred and twenty half-pint mugs of cocoa, and two pint mugs of ditto, the property of Messrs. Clinch and Nippit, assistant teachers, and formerly, report said, sons of decayed shopkeepers themselves. He sat at his desk in the school-room from nine till twelve bullying and browbeating us; he peeped from an upstair window at us in the airing-yard—it was called a play-ground—oh, yes!—he superintended the afternoon lessons till "chastising hour,"—(all offenders were polished off at exactly three in the afternoon to the minute); he had tea with us; he flitted in and out of the room wherein we sat and conned our lessons for the morrow; he saw us up to bed, and when we took a walk with one hundred and twenty specimens of the feminine gender in advance he marched by the male train, and scanned our corduroy ranks with a green and military eye.

Mr. Maxon was a precise man also. It threw him into a bad temper for the entire day if prayers were not read in the school-room precisely as the clock struck nine, and woe betide the unhappy son of a decayed shopkeeper if he were not as punctual as his master ! He saw that breakfast, dinner, and tea were served to the instant—two minutes delay would have insured dismissal of every cook and kitchen wench in the establishment; and he was even known to flog one boy for not going to sleep with the rest at exactly a quarter to seven, when prayers had been read, and one hundred and nineteen youths had sought the companionship of Morpheus.

Mr. Maxon had but one pet in the school, one idol of his heart and apple of his eye, one favourite whom he loved on account of its resemblance to himself—for it was regular to a minute, it never stopped working, it never lost time, and it struck. That object of regard was an old-fashioned clock, which was fixed over the school-room door, and stared Mr. Maxon in the face when he sat at the end of the room.

There was not a boy in the school who regarded that clock with a friendly eye—it had an alarum that could be heard a quarter of a mile off, and that alarum roused the boys at half-past five—it had a sepulchral tick-tick, which was depressing to the spirits—it had never been too fast within the memory of the oldest inhabitant—its warning notes of three, when Mr. Maxon took his life-preserver cane from a peg in the wall, had vibrated in the stoniest heart ; it was, take it for all in all, an ugly humped-backed clock to look at, and the very partiality evinced for it by our stern preceptor set every child of every decayed London shopkeeper against it. It was a peculiar clock too—not a six-day clock or an eight-day clock, but one that required winding up exactly every seven days, an operation which Mr. Maxon performed in

the presence of the school, at five minutes to nine every Monday morning; and
he showed more affection to it during the
ceremony than he had ever testified to one
living soul in corduroy and buttons. When
he was standing on the school-room steps,
he looked the clock smilingly in the face, as
he screwed it up for a week; after which
performance he blew gently and kindly at
the dust, and wiped the glass with the tender
air of a father; and as he returned the key
to its place over the figure XII, he did it
with a sigh, as though winding up clocks
were the most delightful occupation of his
life, and perhaps it was.

Many a time in sour moments have I
watched this Maxon reverence for the time-
piece, and felt inclined to sidle from my
form, and with a determined rush at his
legs, have him off the steps.

When visitors came to the school, Mr.
Maxon always pointed to the clock as the
primary object of attraction.

"That clock, ladies and gentlemen," Mr. Maxon would say, with the air of a show-man, "has been in this school for thirty years, and has not been known to lose a single minute. It has been wound up regularly, and has kept time regularly—silence, you boys there!—from the first moment it was set in its place until this hour. It was the gift of Sheriff Gobble."

There was not a boy in the school on whom Mr. Maxon had a grain of commendation to bestow—not one show-boy to step from his place and astonish the visitors with his general knowledge. He waved his hand towards us when there was company in the school-room, and said "The boys," and I am sure when he took the visitors to the farm-yard—for there was a kind of farm-yard in the rear of the premises—he said "The pigs" with a greater degree of feeling.

I am conscious of a bitter vein running in these lines when I mention my preceptor, but somehow the schoolboy feeling returns

with the years I have retraced, and Mr.
Maxon, in the flesh, again scowls from his
desk at me. .Mr. Maxon and I did not agree
together; from the day of my installation
he seemed, to my boyish, jealous fancy,
to single me out for punishment and severe
example; he never gave me a good word;
when I said my lessons accurately, he shut
the book, and flung it at me; and when I,
more often, said them indifferently, he
appeared to lay on to me at three o'clock
with a degree of relish more satisfactory to
himself than me.

I believe, now, that I was rather more
self-willed than the majority of my contemporaries, more spirited, less able to sub-
mit to harsh dictation. Kind words would
have led me—have led me since in harder
trials—but not all the sternness of a Maxon
could drive me where I did not choose.
Perhaps I was not fit for the school; I was
not a submissive youth; I had been my own
master three years (for my father died when

I was nine years of age, and my mother was a loving mother, who gave me my own way), my life had been a free life in the streets, with street companions, and my nature was not to be suddenly transformed because the school-gates had shut against me and my liberty.

I was a pugnacious boy, too, and got flogged for fighting. I was a climbing boy also, and got flogged for mounting to the top of the play-ground wall, among the broken bottles, and tearing my corduroy trousers in an awful and unseemly manner. I was, moreover, an idle boy, a stubborn boy, and a rebellious boy, and therefore, naturally enough, "Master Burles" came in for a fair share of the three o'clock honours and awards.

One hundred and eighteen boys were pretty docile and teachable ; they said their lessons sometimes, and were praised sometimes, were obedient to Mr. Maxon and assistants generally, and were not particularly distinguished for good or bad behaviour. But Master Burles was one exception, and Master Wilks was another. Birds of a feather have the peculiar habit of flocking together, it is said, and Master Burles struck up a friendship with Master Wilks, after a fight had occurred between them in the airing-ground on the second day of my novitiate, in which contest the writer of this story came off the vanquished, and lost his front tooth.

Master Wilks was one year my senior, a sharp, active youth, who, despite his corduroys and buttons, was quite a handsome-looking boy. He was a noble boy, who never told against a comrade, in or out of school, like other sneaks I knew of; a lively boy, too, not to be depressed by the rules of the establishment, or the scowls of the head-master. He was flogged, upon the average, four times a week, and had not been known once to shed a tear; and he was as full of mischief as any monkey in the Zoological Gardens, Regent's

Park. His little crib in the large dormi-
tories was next to mine, and after Maxon
had taken a survey of us, and made sure
that all our eyes were shut, Wilks and I
used to lie and concoct schemes for the
morrow, or talk of bygone times, when we
were free boys, and our respective parents'
decay had not commenced. Occasionally
we talked of our mothers—he had a widowed mother as well as I, and I believe that
coincidence helped to draw us closer to each
other. " His mother was very, very poor,"
he used to say, " and had to keep herself
and his little sister out of the profits of a
chandler's-shop at Camberwell. He should
never forget how pleased his mother was
when he got in, after the tenth application;
and how pleased he was too, for her sake,
though he had been praying inwardly all
day that some one would get in instead of
him." He talked of his sister occasionally,
and wished that I could see her, and she
could see me, especially when she and I

were grown up, and were able to marry each other, and start a chandler's business like his mother's.

"It wasn't always a chandler's-shop life, Dick," he would say to me sometimes. "When my father was alive, he had a plate-glass shop in the City, and lots of carriage customers, I can tell you."

Then we whispered of the past and better times, and Mr. Nippit, who slept in a crib of larger dimensions than ours, at the end of the room—Room No. 1, East Wing—seldom tried to stop us, for he was a good sort, and everybody thought so.

I had not been three months in the institution, before I was reported to the Board, and had up to the Board, too (which sat once in three weeks), to receive a stern reprimand from several stout old gentlemen at a green-baize table. That was an awful trial to face the grave faces, and receive a terrible reproof, and a heap of Scriptural quotations; but I got used to it after the third time, especially as Master Robert Wilks—I always called him Bob Wilks myself—did me the honour to accompany me. Bob and I always promised to be good boys—that was but common civility—and we tried, too, sometimes, for three whole days; but at the end of six weeks, at furthest, there we were again!

At last the Board, tired with our constant appearance in the same characters, and prejudiced by the stern reports of Mr. Maxon, informed us that the next flagrant act of disobedience which led to our summons before the Council would be followed by our ignominious dismissal from the school. This decision was communicated to our mothers; and our mothers, in great distress of mind, called to see us on the day set apart for maternal and paternal visits, and begged us—Bob's mother on her knees—to be good boys, and learn our lessons, and be dutiful to our teachers and masters, for their sakes, and for the credit of those good ladies and gentlemen whose votes had helped to place us in the school.

These maternal appeals preyed upon Bob Wilks and me, and set us thinking. Bob was more impressed than I, for his mother had been more energetic, and he scratched his head, hitched up his corduroys, and said to me, under cover of his copy-book, that afternoon,

" Here goes for a new leaf to-morrow, Dick—it'll never do to break my old mother's heart."

From that day Wilks steadily improved; he worked at his lessons, played only at allotted seasons, abjured practical jokes, and astonished even Maxon with his reformation. I endeavoured to imitate Bob, for I knew that no greater misfortune could happen to my mother than my expulsion from the school; and, as the natural result of my efforts, my place in the class approached more closely to the top, and my name at three o'clock was called out less often.

Still I did not gain ground in the esteem of the amiable Maxon; he seemed rather put out, I fancied, by my attempts at reformation, and did his best to keep me a bad boy. He never gave me a word of praise or encouragement, he was always suspecting me, he called out once or twice a day in a stentorian voice, "I see you, Burles," when there was nothing to see but a bullet-headed boy hard at work with slate and pencil.

But all work and no play made Dick a dull boy; the picture of my tear-stained mother's face got three weeks old, and I was growing tired of routine, and sick of every lesson; working at my sums without mistakes, and at my writing-lessons without blots, became a monotonous occupation that did not agree with my constitution. I was becoming pale in consequence, and my corduroy breeches hung more loosely on my limbs.

I gave vent to my suppressed feelings one Sunday afternoon, and, in the words of

Master Wilks, "did it nicely." I have already alluded to our school-walks, when one hundred and twenty boys followed in the rear of one hundred and twenty girls, and Mr. Maxon, or an assistant-teacher, formed the escort of our particular gender. One Sunday and wintry afternoon, then, after some days of heavy rain, Mr. Maxon took advantage of a burst of sunshine to order out the school. Girls and boys having washed their faces, and put on their caps and bonnets, were ordered out accordingly. The country was looking delightful after five days confinement within the institution walls; the air blew sweet and fresh; the ground was inclined to be muddy; Mr. Maxon, as usual, disposed to be snappish; Messrs. Wilks and Burles rather disposed to be facetious. Master Wilks endeavoured to check his flow of spirits, and succeeded; Master Burles, with less moral resolution, made the same attempt, and succeeded not.

Now the two boys walking immediately

in advance of me and Wilks were brothers, twins, red-haired, and the biggest cowards in the school; the two boys following us were boys of our own species, boys fond of a little fun, when they were *quite* sure Mr. Maxon was looking another way. The boys behind, taking advantage of Mr. Maxon's attention to the smaller fry, twenty yards off, trod playfully on the heels of myself and friend—self and friend, desirous of passing on the compliment, took the skin off the red-haired brothers in advance—red-haired brothers of the name of Rufus looked round indignantly, and threatened to tell "Master." Master Wilks said, "Do, if you like," but "knuckled under" on the instant; adding, in a whisper, "Board-room, Dick." Dick, having confidence in human nature, rasped the heels of the elder Rufus again, previous to knuckling under also; elder Rufus, not expecting a repetition of the offence after his reprimand, was taken off his guard, gave a jump and a stumble over his own feet, and then—horror of horrors!—fell with a heavy flop on the dirty foot-path, his Sunday cotton gloves grasping spasmodically at a heap of muddy batter which had been carefully scraped together by the roadside.

"Oh! my eye, Dick!" was all Wilks could ejaculate in his terror and amazement.

I felt my heart sink into my thick-soled high-lows, as George Rufus burst into terrific howls, and the shout of Maxon's "HALT!" thundered in my ears.

"Halt, you boys! Rufus, you young wretch, get out of that mud! *Who* has done this?—WHO has done this? I—I—I'll be the death of him!"

White with passion, Mr. Maxon advanced towards us, shaking his fists, stamping his feet, and scarcely able to articulate in his vehemence. Master Rufus, with a black "gorm" down his shirt front, waistcoat, and corduroys, with his nose bleeding, and the peak of his cap damaged, gathered himself together, went bellowing back to his place in the ranks, and stood there, shaking little dabs of mud from his brown cotton gloves.

"How dare you fall down, you young vagabond!"

"P—p—please, sir, it was Burles."

"Burles—*Burles*—BURLES, was it!"

I began to feel uncomfortable in my corduroys.

"He kept tread—tread—trea—treading on my heels, and at last he threw me down, sir!" cried Rufus.

"It was quite an accident," I murmured.

"Accident!" shouted Maxon—"you're always doing something!"

Whack came his sledge-hammer hand on my left ear, over I went into the very place which Master Rufus had wiped for me, up I came again, supported by the hand of Mr. Maxon on the collar of my jacket.

"You did that on purpose—you know you did!" cried Maxon, varying the proceedings by a shake.

"No, I didn't!" I vociferated.

Mr. Maxon relaxed his hold.

"Turn back, all of you—you shall go home again for this. Can't proceed with two such dirty beasts as these in the ranks. Burles, as sure as the clock strikes three to-morrow afternoon, I'll give you the soundest flogging that you have ever had in your life. Right about face!"

Leaving the one hundred and twenty girls under the escort of Miss Binks— the boys did say in my time that old Maxon was after Miss Binks—we retraced our steps, two boys of the number certainly depressed in spirits. It may seem strange to say that I was not one of the two, despite to-morrow's threatened punishment. Wilks was dull, and Rufus was still snivelling, and in fear of the life-preserver; but I was more inclined to be savage, there being still all manner of noises in the ear on which the Maxon paw had so ferociously descended.

I was in disgrace the remainder of the day, of course—the boys were forbidden to address a word to me, on pain of Mr. Maxon's severe displeasure, and the still more severe, &c., at three o'clock to-morrow. I had my tea, strictly on the silent system, and I turned into my crib at night, without hearing a syllable of condolence with my misfortunes, even from Bob Wilks.

When Mr. Maxon had taken his last look at the east wing division of the one hundred and twentieth legion, and Mr. Nippit was feigning sleep as usual, and paying no heed to many a muffled voice, Bob Wilks's head peered over the counterpane of the adjoining crib.

" I say, Dick, I'm precious sorry."

" I don't care."

" I hope it won't come before the Board."

" I don't care if it does."

" I was in it as well as you—I don't like you to have all the hiding—it isn't fair, Dick."

" Oh ! never mind me, I'm used to hidings by this time."

" Perhaps he'll forget it," said the sanguine Wilks.

" Oh ! yes, especially when he sees Rufus's nose in the morning."

Wilks disappeared beneath the counter-pane, and a stifled choking was heard im-mediately to follow.

I always laughed when Wilks laughed, it was a contagious cachinnation—that's a strange word for a scholar like me to get hold of—and there was no resisting it. I was the first to recover from the effects of the joke, the thoughts of next day interfer-ing with my hilarity. When Wilks had risen to the surface, like a trout for air, I said,

" I shan't laugh to-morrow much, Bob."

" No," said Bob, very grave now. " When that infernal clock strikes three won't you feel precious nervous ? What are you jump-ing at ?"

" It shan't strike three !" I ejaculated.

"What?"

"Nothing.　Never mind.　Don't say another word, there's a good fellow.　Good night."

"Good night.　I say, Dick!"

"What is it now?"

"There's an old copy-book of mine in the locker.　I should put it on to-morrow before the corduroys."

"All right, Bob.　Thankee."

"Order there.　Who *is* that talking?" cried the feeble voice of Nippit.

Nippit knew as well as we did, though he feigned perfect ignorance.

"I shall put some of your names down for to-morrow's task-book, if you boys can't behave yourselves."

He did not mean it; he would as soon have dreamed of obtaining sixty pounds a year salary as of getting one of his flock into disgrace; but we respected his wishes, and held our tongues. Wilks and the boys went to sleep, Nippit began to snore, and I to grow more wide awake and thoughtful.

"*As sure as the clock strikes three to-morrow afternoon, I'll give you the soundest flogging that you have ever had in your life!*"

I lay and bit my nails, and the bed-clothes, and then my nails again, and turned this threat over and over in my mind till half-past eleven o'clock at night.

"Why did he not pitch into me this afternoon, and have it out? Why doesn't he always cane a boy at once, and not leave it for hours and hours to prey upon his brain, and worry him? As sure as his clock strikes three, indeed! Hang his dirty, old-fashioned, hump-backed clock!"

I sprang up in bed. "It shan't strike three! I told Bob so, and it shan't!" I looked round; the night-lamp in the fireplace was burning faintly, all the boys were fast asleep, and Mr. Nippit was indulging in an imaginary gargle, with his head hanging over his crib. All manner of thoughts, daring, wicked thoughts, came trooping to my mind; to set the school on fire; to run away in my little night-shirt, and leave my corduroys behind me; to feign an attack of raving madness, and horrify the school, and rush at Maxon and bite him, if I got a chance; to stop the clock, and hide the key!

To hide the key! That would succeed admirably, for Mr. Maxon's day for winding up was Monday, and if he missed the key he could not wind it up; and if he could not wind it up, it would stop in the course of the morning; and if it stopped in the course of the morning, why, it was not as sure as the clock struck three that I should be flogged, for it would not strike three at all. Here goes!

I was out of bed and sneaking into my corduroys as silently as possible. I did not wait for socks or shoes, but stole barefooted to the door, opened it noiselessly, slipped into the passage, and ran paddling down the stairs. I knew my way in the dark as well as Miss Binks's cat, and instinct guided me to the lonely school-room. How the abhorred tick, tick, tick began to welcome me as I pushed open the door! Pitch dark, and the steps the Lord knows where! Groping among the forms and along by the wall, and bringing my head with a smash against Mr. Maxon's desk. Fighting my way back among the forms again, stumbling towards Mr. Clinch's official post, and final discovery of the steps behind the school-room door. I sat down on them triumphantly, and re-covered breath for the first *coup-de-main.*

Tick, tick, tick, defiantly. I proceeded to arrange the steps beneath the clock; I began to make my perilous ascent.

Short by two feet! By standing on the tips of my very cold toes, I could just touch the bottom of the clock—with an effort I might have opened the trap and stolen the pendulum, but that article was not conveni-ent to hide, and in my efforts to dislodge it, I might bring down myself, the clock, and the

steps in one general ruin.   I descended,
opened the nearest locker—our lockers, the
reader will please to understand, were deep
receptacles for books made in the heavy
school-forms, an economic disposal of space
still in fashion at a few large schools—and
taking out several books placed them on the
steps.   The contents of locker No. 2, added
to the store in locker No. 3, completed the
shaky pyramid, on which I mounted like a
young Italian "bounding brother." The books
rocked with my weight; I felt one or two of
the little ones slipping away.   I touched the
clock, stood on tiptoe, made a snatch along
the top, gained the key, and sprang to the
floor, just too late to save the first half-dozen
books from falling to the floor with an awful crash.

I gave myself up for lost, and stood shaking
in every limb, and waiting for doors to open
and feet to come hurrying down the stairs.
All silent, the clock tick, ticking in the old
sepulchral fashion; not a hinge creaking in

the distance, not a single being in the Institution for the children of decayed London shopkeepers aroused to life and action by my blunder. I gathered courage, groped on the floor for the books, and bundled them back into the lockers, the lids of which I had left open for that purpose. After taking the remaining volumes off the steps and dropping them also into the lockers, I wheeled the steps behind the door, and flitted upstairs in a ghost-like manner.

I pushed open the door of No. 1, east wing. The light was still glimmering. Mr. Nippit had left off gargling, and his head had got further out of bed. Bob Wilks was dreaming about the Board Room, and saying in his sleep that he would never do it again. The remaining boys were in blissful ignorance of the shivering youth who came stealing into the room at the witching hour of night. Exactly midnight, for that clock down stairs began to strike as I crept between the sheets. I was glad it had not struck before.   I felt that, if it had struck twelve whilst my hand was on the top feeling for the key, I should have fallen off the steps in a fit.   Feeling for the key— the key!   I sat up in bed once more, and held my head between my hands. The key! —what had I done with the key? I put my hand out of bed, dragged my corduroys to- wards me, and felt nervously in the pockets. Not there—GONE!

Where was it?   I had taken it off the clock when I had jumped to the ground; I had been paralysed with fear some mo- ments after the fall of the books; I had put the books back in the lockers, but what had I done with the key?   I did not remember having the key in my hands when I groped about the floor for the books—I remembered nothing! I gave it up as a bad job—it would not do to risk going downstairs again to the schoolroom, and searching in the dark for the key; if it were found on the floor in the morning, Mr. Maxon would suppose that it had fallen off the clock in the night, and there was an end of my trouble—that is, of that sort of trouble. I put my corduroys back with a sigh, lay down in bed, turned my face from the night light, and slept soundly till the alarum of the enemy roused me with the early dawn.

Ten minutes to nine that Monday morning was not a pleasant time for me; the boys were getting into their places and opening their lockers, Maxon with the life-preserver cane under his arm was coming into school. Mr. Maxon, after strutting to the end of the room and hanging up his life-preserver, turned his back to the fire, and stood with his coat-tails gracefully tucked under his arms.

" What is the reason for all that disturb-ance at the lockers ?" was his first inquiry. " Speak up some of you !"

" Can't find my grammar, sir," whimpered one.

"Here's Matthew's spelling-book in my locker, sir," cried another.

"Matthews," said Mr. Maxon sternly, "you will please to learn an extra column of spelling before dinner. That will teach you to keep your books in the right place."

"I didn't put the book there, sir," cried Matthews.

"You will say two columns for rudely contradicting me."

Matthews the wronged burst into tears.

Five minutes to nine—Mr. Maxon dropped his coat tails, walked pompously along the school-room, advanced to the steps, and settled them beneath the clock. The boys were in their places, the mistakes of the books had been corrected, and Mr. Maxon, punctual to a minute, was on the steps ready to wind up the clock! I turned my head to the charmed spot and watched the proceeding behind my "Lessons in Geography." One or two boys followed my example, in an indolent manner that was a strange contrast to

my own rapt attention—the rest were hum-
ming over their tasks, and freshening up
their memories from Saturday-night's study.

Mr. Maxon puffed away the seven days'
accumulation of dust, looked the clock affec-
tionately in the face, wiped the glass, as usual,
with his pocket-handkerchief, compared the
time with his own silver frying-pan, opened
the glass, raised his hand and gently glided
it towards the well-known resting-place of
THE KEY!

A pause—the hand a second time passed
carefully over the top of the clock, and
then in an absent dreamy manner over the
Maxon forehead, which it marked with five
fine smutches. Another pause—Mr. Maxon,
still unable to credit his senses, repeated the
movement, gave a faint cough, then a loud
one, turned round, descended, looked
anxiously right and left and under the steps,
scratched his head, ran up the steps lamp-
lighter fashion once more, and standing on
tiptoe gazed at the top of the clock.

Yes, it was gone; the awful truth dawned upon him slowly. He stood staring at the clock, and one hundred and nineteen boys, whose curiosity had been awakened by his strange proceedings, sat with their heads over their shoulders watching him. Mr. Maxon gave a little jump, acrobat-fashion, on the top step, and faced his pupils.

"What are you looking at?" he roared.

The heads were in natural position again; there was an intense application to the lessons of the day. Cough the third—a tremendous cough this time.

"*Ahem!* Have any of you boys seen a key—a clock key—the key of *this* clock?"

"No, sir!" shouted a hundred and nineteen voices.

"Have you, Mr. Nippit—Mr. Clinch?"

"No, sir," was the simultaneous response.

"I hope neither you nor Mr. Clinch has attempted to wind up this clock."

"Oh! no, sir."

"And mislaid the key afterwards," looking daggers at Mr. Clinch, of whom he was evidently suspicious.

"Should never dream of taking such a liberty, sir," said Mr. Clinch.

"You'd better not."

Clinch coloured to the roots of his hair, but made no reply. He had the heart to be uncivil—I saw it in his face—but he swallowed his desire, and looked up at the ceiling.

Mr. Maxon, growing more intensely savage as the importance of his loss began to prey upon him, put his hands in his trouser pockets, and swaggered down the steps with thunder on his countenance.

"Have any of you boys seen the key of the clock ?"

General and deafening shout of "No, sir !"

"The school will remain till half-past twelve this morning," said Maxon, vindictively, "for making such an abominable uproar."

A rapid interchange of blank looks.

"It's very annoying and exceedingly strange," he muttered, as he took his seat. "I placed the key there myself—I've placed it in the same place for twenty-five years nearly, and now it's gone! Some of you boys"—in a louder voice, accompanied with one of his heavy bangs on the desk—"MUST have seen that key!"

No one answered—no one evidently had seen it. I could have risen in my place with my hand upon my heart, and said, "Mr. Maxon, I, Richard Burles, have not *seen* the key of the clock."

"I—I—I—I'll sift to the bottom of all this, mind you," cried Maxon; "it never went without hands, and if—if—if I only find who's done it, I'll——"

BANG! The clock struck nine, and Mr. Maxon, scowling like an ogre, writhed upon his chair. There was his clock, at nine in the morning, unwound for the first time—that punctual and extraordinary clock!

It would run down—it would get out of order; there was not a clockmaker within five miles, and there was no one could be spared to go in search of him till the boys were in their beds. Then it was a peculiar clock—required a peculiarly-shaped key— ten chances to one if a key had not to be made for it, and the clock sent to London in consequence.

" Mr. Nippit, will you go to Miss Binks, and ask her if she knows anything of this sad affair ?"

" Yes, sir."

A gloomy silence, till the return of Mr. Nippit, with Miss Binks's compliments, and she had not seen the key.

Mr. Moxon ground his teeth, and gave another bang to his desk.

" And what did Perkins say, Mr. Nippit?"

" Perkins, sir ?"

Perkins was a maid-of-all-work, in the habit of sweeping out the school-room every morning.

"I don't think you told me to ask Perkins, sir."

"I did, sir." (Bang, bang!) "It's uncommonly hard, sir, to have to do with stupid people, who can't take their orders correctly. Don't stand there like a stuck pig, sir. Go and ask Perkins directly."

Mr. Nippit skulked out of the room, and took his crestfallen countenance into the kitchen of the establishment.

Mr. Maxon sat and played an irritating tattoo on his desk till the return of Mr. Nippit.

" Well, sir ?"

" Perkins has seen nothing of a key, Mr. Maxon."

"Nothing of a key !" mimicking Mr. Nippit's falsetto. "What do you mean, sir, by bringing me such a ridiculous message as that? It's *something* of a key, sir,—the key of that clock, sir!" The bang that followed this nearly split the desk in two.

"Perkins says she noticed the room was

out of order, just under the clock, sir. She picked up a spelling-book, a sheet of paper, and some old quill pens."

"Couldn't you have told me that before, Mr. Nippit?"

"I told you as quick as I could, sir," said Mr. Nippit, with an elevation of voice, "and I couldn't tell you any sooner."

"Very well, sir!—very well!" said Mr. Maxon, as his subordinate walked back to his desk. "Pretty behaviour from a junior usher, and a very nice example of respect and civility for the boys to copy. I shall report you to the Board, sir."

Mr. Nippit opened his desk and began rummaging therein in a violent manner.

"And where is this book that was picked up?" (Bang!)

"Put back in the locker," answered Nippit.

"Whose?"

"Wilks's, sir," was the reluctant reply.

"WILKS," with a tremendous roar,

"do you know anything about the key?"

"No, sir."

"You do—you know you do—you're laughing!"

"No, I ain't, sir."

"How came your spelling-book under the clock, Wilks? It wasn't there Saturday night, and you haven't had it since."

"Somebody's been to my locker, sir. It's in an awful mess, and——"

"If you say another word, I'll skin you alive! Prayers, you imps!"

Up started the one hundred and twenty boys, and Mr. Maxon, in far from a heavenly humour, commenced reading the prayers for that particular day of the month, according to a custom still in use at the Decayed Shopkeepers' Children's Asylum, though Mr. Maxon, of that establishment, has long since relinquished his devotions, and is past all praying for.

Mr. Maxon's temper did not soften down during his readings; he could not get the

key of the clock out of his head, and the
remembrance kept his blood at fever-heat.
He prayed between his set teeth, and glared
at the boys with fiery eyes, and wondered
which of the one hundred and twenty had
stolen the key of his favourite time-piece.

School began, lessons were recited, whole
classes were turned back, everybody was
in fault, everybody was in a state of
great nervous excitement. Nothing went
on well, of course. The spelling-class was
half an hour behind time, the geography
class was threatened with annihilation;
Master Wilks was to have no dinner for
losing his place in his reading-lesson; Master Burles was promised three choice and
distinct canings, in addition to the one already down to his credit, for not knowing
a word of his lessons; and——the clock
stopped at a quarter past eleven!

That last incident was the feather on the
overburdened camel's back. Mr. Maxon
went out of his mind. How he banged

the desk after that calamity!—how he roared at the boys, and at the ushers, and at a little girl who came in from Miss Binks and wanted to know what time it was, as Miss Binks was sure *her* clock wasn't right.

The morning passed, and we were dismissed at half-past twelve by Mr. Maxon's watch, which was about five-and-twenty minutes too fast. After dinner we strayed into the airing or play-ground, and stood in little knots, and talked of the missing key. Wilks, who had had no dinner, came towards me, and asked in a husky whisper whether I knew anything concerning it.

"How should I know, Bob?"

"You said it shouldn't strike, if you remember?"

"That was only my fun."

"Then you didn't?"

"And didn't you, Bob?"

Bob looked at me and laughed. How he enjoyed the joke, though he had turned over a new leaf, and become such a good boy.

"If you don't tell me, Dick, I shan't know anything about it, shall I ?"

"Of course you won't."

" What a fellow you are, Dick ! and what a lark this is ! I like this better than the dinner I haven't had—a precious sight !"

Ring, ring, ring, ring, ring, ring, RING.

" Hollo ! it isn't two o'clock, Dick. What's the matter ?"

" I can't tell. We're rung in, that's certain. Perhaps old Maxon thinks it *is* two ; the clock's stopped, you know."

We exchanged broad grins as we ran towards the school-room with the rest of the boys. We soon left off grinning when we saw Mr. Maxon at his desk, holding in his hand the key of the clock !

" In your places !" he shouted.

How my knees knocked together as I took my place by the side of Wilks ! It was all up—I was in for it—I could see the eyes of Maxon fixed in my direction. Thoughts of my poor mother, who had striven so hard to get me in—of the Board-room—the stern old gentlemen and the table with the green baize—of the hours that were numbered—of the small innings I had had for my game.

" Which boy owns to taking this ?" *Bang.*

I did not answer, and the one hundred and nineteen were silent also, naturally enough.

" *Which boy ?*"

No answer.

" Wilks, do you ?"

" No, sir," said Wilks boldly.

Mr. Maxon went off like a bomb-shell. He exploded with a series of the most dreadful bangs upon his desk. No frantic drummer could have equalled him ; he stamped with both feet ; he tossed his head about, and foamed wildly at the mouth ; he fought and struggled with his utterance.

He found his voice at last.

"You wicked, lying, thieving young vagabond !—you scum of the earth, you wretched, depraved, insolent, traitorous, rebellious
young villain !—you—you everything that
is bad—and worse—come out !"

"*Me*, sir !" exclaimed Master Wilks.

"Come out !—come out !" cried he,
flourishing the hand with a key in it ; "and
don't stand *me*-ing me ! Come out !" *Bang !*

Bob left his place, and walked towards
Mr. Maxon's desk.

"Stand there, and take your hands out of
your pockets."

Bob was all obedience.

"Now, do you know where this came
from ?" hitting Master Wilks on the nose
with the key as he spoke.

"No, sir," said Bob, winking his eyelids
once or twice.

" *No, sir !*" echoed Maxon, making another
dash at his nose with the same instrument,
which Bob evaded by ducking his head,
much to Mr. Maxon's indignation, who

knocked him down for not standing still.

When Bob Wilks and Mr. Maxon were face to face again, Mr. Maxon repeated the " No, SIR !"

" No, sir," again said Bob.

Bang, *bang*, BANG on the desk.

" It was in your locker, sir !"

Bob turned pale.

" At the bottom—carefully hidden, of course—at the bottom of your locker, sir ; and what have you to say to that ?"

" I didn't put it there."

" It's a lie, sir !"

" No, it's not, sir."

Down went Bob again.

" How dare you contradict me by these disgraceful falsehoods ?"

" I didn't put it there," repeated Bob, who was still on his back, and probably did not see the advantage of changing his position.

" Who did ?" cried Maxon.

I doubled myself into a small heap, and

my heart began thumping against my ribs in fine style.

" I—I don't know, sir."

" Of course you don't," ironically.

" No one told me about taking the key of the clock, or of putting it in my desk, and——"

"Get up, and don't lie there!" cried Maxon, with a kick at the prostrate Bob—"go to your seat, do! I shall not punish you, Wilks—this is too flagrant a case for me to dispose of—I shall report you to the Board."

"Oh! don't do that, sir!" cried Wilks, jumping to his feet; " you may flog me as much as you like, and keep me without my dinners till I go away for good, and kick me ever so much, and knock my nose off with that key, but don't report me to the Board again, please."

" Go to your seat."

"I didn't do it—upon my word and honour, I didn't take the key."

" Who did ?"

Bob's chest heaved, and his hands tightened, and I saw his eyes for a moment fixed in my direction.

" I don't know," said Bob, after a long and awful pause.

" I'll tell you, then," said Maxon, " Robert Wilks, boy of the second class, reported to the Board which sits next Wednesday."

Bob walked to his seat, opened his book, thrust his hands to the lowest depths of his corduroys, and stared at the page before him.　He did not trust himself to look at me, who sat beside him with a white face, and a beating heart that was tortured with remorse.　All the rest of the day he never spoke one word to me, did not even console me after my three o'clock floggings—the accursed clock struck, after all !—but sat staring at his book till he was called with his class, and resumed his position again after the class had been dismissed.

Bob was very dull at tea, and even at

bed-time he turned into his crib without a word to me. When all was quiet for the night, and Nippit was gargling as usual, I whispered—

"Bob."

No answer was returned.

"Are you asleep, Bob?"

"No."

"I'm so sorry—I never meant the key should be found, of course. I must have put it in the locker with the books, for I lost it when——"

"Don't tell me anything about it, Dick—it can't be helped now. Don't say any more ; I shan't split !"

"But——"

"Please don't talk—my head aches."

He would not answer when I called his name a second time, so I lay speculating as to what would be the end of it all, and whether Bob—poor old innocent Bob!—would be turned out of school for a fault that he had never committed. I thought

"What if I were to confess?" Then my heart stopped at the thought, for my mother was very poor, and had striven hard to place me where I was. Oh! dear, perhaps Bob's mother would not take it so much to heart as mine, for Bob was older and bigger than I, and better able to work his way in the world.

The next day was an awful heart-breaking day. Bob was very pale, and absent in his manner; he said his lessons worse than ever, and was flogged at three o'clock for his sins of omission.

"Instead of being a good boy to-day—your last day in this school, most probably," cried Mr. Maxon, as he laid on to him briskly at three o'clock, "you don't repeat a single lesson correctly. You make up your mind to annoy me and everybody else—you're a reckless and abandoned boy."

Bob looked it when he got back to his place, and sat with his hands in his pockets after the old fashion, and with a dogged, evil cast of countenance, which was after a new fashion that I had never seen before.

Wednesday, Board-room day—Bob Wilks's day. At eleven o'clock in the morning, Mr. Maxon, who had been previously sent for, made his appearance, and walked slowly down the school-room. I knew what was coming; I was shaking with a forty horse-power. I glanced at Bob, he seemed as cool as ever, but the dogged look was more apparent.

"Wilks," cried Maxon, "the Board wants you. Come along with me."

"I'm coming, sir."

Bob looked at me, and muttered, as he rose—

"You need not be afraid, Dick."

He joined Mr. Maxon, and master and scholar walked side by side towards the door. As they neared the end of the school-room, I, who had not taken my eyes from them, rose to my feet, stood even on the form, in my anxiety to keep them in sight.

"Burles," cried Messrs. Nippit and Clinch in one breath, "what are you doing, sir? What's the matter with you?"

They were at the door. Mr. Maxon's hand had already opened it; but Wilks looked round and met my gaze.

"MR. MAXON!" I shrieked.

The boys jumped in their seats; a scared look was on everybody's face; Mr. Maxon turned quite pale. I sprang off the form, tumbled over the boys in my frantic eagerness, rushed along the school-room, and caught the astonished Master Wilks round the waist.

"He shan't go—he didn't do it—he didn't do it!" I cried. "Just let him go, and take me instead. I stole the key of the clock, and put it in his locker. I did it in the night; it wasn't Wilks, indeed, sir."

"You—you—it was you, then?" gasped Maxon.

"Yes, sir—only me. Bob—Master Wilks knew nothing of it."

"Oh! Dick, why did you tell?" cried Bob.

" Stay here," said Mr. Maxon.

The schoolmaster left us standing by the door, went to his desk, wrote out a second report, in which my name figured conspicuously, came back with it in his right hand, and took my own hand in his left.

" You can return to your seat," said Mr. Maxon to Bob; " I will account for your non-appearance. Go back, sir; it's a very lucky escape for you."

I don't know that there is any more to say about this key; the rest is rather painful, is not worth dwelling on, and says little for the kindness of human nature.

Mr. Maxon accounted to the terrible Board for the mistake of names, substituted my corporeal frame for that of Master Wilks, but did not explain the means by which I stood his substitute, dwelt on my general vices, and the enormity of the offence for which I stood there a prisoner a great deal, and said little of the rescue of my school companion.   And what had I to say ?   I did it—there was no denying *that ;* I was one black sheep in the flock, and if I had tried to wash myself white before the Board, the Board would not have stayed for the experiment.   There was nothing to say, and Richard Burles was found guilty, sentenced, EXPELLED.   Perhaps they did right —perhaps they did wrong.   I did not feel sorry for confessing all that I knew about the key—not even when my broken-hearted mother came to take me home, and the doors of the Institution for the Children of Decayed Shopkeepers banged against me for the last time, and shut Bob Wilks's face away from mine for ever.

FRIEND KARL.

FRIEND KARL.

WHY I should have taken to Karl Ehrhardt it is not an easy matter to explain. There was but little in common between us, except the profession to which we both belonged, and which was an up-hill, struggling profession then with both of us. He was impatient, irritable, and in his way a vain man; I was quiet, methodical, and cool. He was dissatisfied with his progress at the outset of his career; I was content to wait, as better men had done before me, and to hope in good time for a fair share of the prizes. His was an ambition that heated his blood, and kept him restless; mine was an ambition that I tried to hide, lest those less sanguine than myself should laugh at the wild dreams I had. He was a German, without that stolidity which marks at times the German character; I was an Englishman, possibly more deliberate than most of my countrymen. I was fond of society, and he detested it; I had mother, father, brothers, and sisters living then, and he was a man alone in the world.

But we were both painters, and we were both poor. My father was a clergyman in the West of England—a man with a small living and a large family; and when, very early in life, I chose my out-of-the-way trade, as my father called it, perhaps a little contemptuously, I felt that I was reducing the family expenses, and so acting for the good of that family of which I was proud.

We had served our apprenticeship to art when we became first acquainted with each other. I was three-and-twenty years of age, and he was seven years my senior. We were known in certain odd corners as men at least handy with our pencils. There was a painting of mine upon the walls of the Royal Academy that year, and the critics had given it a line or two of praise; and Karl Ehrhardt had been offered an engagement to illustrate a leading magazine, and had accepted it.

It was in a Welsh mountain pass that we first met. We had each stolen a holiday in the bright days of July; and, like prudent men, were making even holidays profitable by sketching on the way. I remember that on this particular occasion I had been attracted by a bold bit of landscape—a weird rock-piece, shadowed by the larches—and was roughly sketching it in my note-book when he came along the hill-side, and paused at a little distance from me.

He appeared surprised to see me—though the pass was a well-known one, and a short cut to a famous mountain district, where tourists were always thick in Summer time

—and he hesitated for an instant, as if my appearance there, or the task upon which I was engaged, demanded a little explanation. He advanced to my side at last, and looked impatiently over my shoulder at the sketch that I was making.

"You have chosen a bad subject, sir," he said suddenly. "That is a harsh piece of Welsh landscape, which will not repay you for your trouble. Further along the pass you will find some admirable bits of colour."

I thanked him for his information, but went on with my sketch. The subject had become of greater interest as it had grown more familiar to me, and I had resolved to return to the spot later in the day, when the glow of the sunset was upon it, and colour in the scene.

Meanwhile I went on with my picture, and Karl Ehrhardt watched me for awhile, and then turned away, and went further along the pass.

Later that day, when the sunset had

flushed the rock with crimson, I returned,
to find my late adviser planted at a short
distance from the spot which I had previously occupied, and engaged in reproducing on
his canvas an elaborate painting of that very
scene which he had condemned as a harsh
bit of landscape in the morning.

He was intent on his task, and did not
observe my approach; my voice startled
him, and he looked round fiercely at me
when I bade him good evening.

"This takes your fancy, then?" he said,
with some degree of energy. "What is
there in it that you should like, or care to
paint, with all this wealth of Nature round
you from which to choose?"

"The rock is fanciful; that tree, springing
from the cleft like a something that has
struggled for its freedom to the light, pleases
me immensely."

"You are a poet, perhaps?" he said,
sneeringly.

"No, an artist, like yourself."

"How easy it is to say artist!" was his curt reply.

"Ah! and how hard to get others to acknowledge that you are one!"

"Exactly."

We were silent for awhile, and I regarded more attentively the uncivil being who objected to my course of studies. He was a man some inches shorter than myself, a frail, thin, sallow-faced man, with eyes and hair as black as night—a man whom, at first sight, one would have taken for a Spaniard rather than a German. A very sad countenance it was in repose, I thought; and if the heart was as full of gloom, he was one who looked at life as from a dungeon wherein he was a prisoner.

It was that melancholy face which first attracted me towards him; and the suppressed anger upon it when he looked at me did not deter me from my fancies. He was one, I thought, of whom I should like to know more; evidently an eccentric, and, possibly, an uncommon man.

As I opened my colour-box, and sat down at a short distance from him, I noticed that he furtively regarded me. When I was painting in my morning's sketch, my persistence in selecting that particular spot for my note-book appeared to irritate him, for he stamped his foot upon the ground, and muttered something to himself.

I ventured to address him again, and after a few minutes' silence.

" It is an odd coincidence that you and I should both have hit upon one study," I said; " for, as you remarked this morning, there are finer bits of colour in the neighbourhood."

He did not answer for several moments. I thought that he was not going to favour me with a reply, when he said at last—

" Yes; it is odd."

" Yours is an elaborate picture, which you probably intend for exhibition."

"Not in this instance.   I am painting for myself."

"Indeed!"

"You," he said, after another pause, "are merely adding to your scrap-book?"

"A rough note by the way.   I may profit by it or not at a future time," I answered, "according to the impression that is left upon me."

"You have travelled?" he asked suddenly.

"A little—in Switzerland and France."

"Only in Switzerland and France?" he added, interrogatively.

And to my reply in the affirmative he said—

"Ah! you should see Italy, if this is likely to be your profession."

"It is my profession already."

He looked surprised for a moment, and then said—

"May I ask your name?"

"Whitfield."

"I do not recognize it; but it takes time —a long time—to be known," he answered. "In these fancy professions, a man gets fame—and then only a lucky man—when fame is of no value to him, and the world wherein he struggles is passing away from him. Oh! if, like Balzac's Russian peasant, this life was a bad dream, and our dreams were reality, how much better it might be for us."

He ceased painting to reflect upon this, and the glow of the sunset had stolen from the rock when he looked up again.

"It is only for a few minutes one catches the sunlight there," he said; "and I have wasted half of them. May I see what you have done?"

I showed him my crude sketch, and he said—

"You have the trick of the colourist, and may succeed in your profession. I am more happy with my pencil."

Before our interview terminated that

evening, I had learned his name, and found that it was not wholly strange to me.   Perhaps I had already begun to feel that liking for the man which occurs once or twice in life to most of us, and is in many instances incapable of explanation.   His manner was variable and strange.   He had accosted me rudely in the first instance, then had grown communicative, and finally had turned away, and walked towards the village, preceding me by a few steps, and not speaking a word.

There were several artists at the inn where we stayed ; it was artists' quarters, and a fair starting-point for the scenery which painters love ; but I discovered the next day that he had made no companions amongst the visitors, and, indeed, had shunned them all with a scrupulosity that was remarkable.

When I told them that Ehrhardt and I had been at work on the same view, and had conversed together for awhile, they congratulated me on having gained an advantage over them, and asked a few questions concerning him, with a carelessness that showed no particular curiosity in my answers, and no great interest in the man who held aloof from them. He had thought himself better than the rest, and after all he was only Ehrhardt the illustrator, and beneath many of them in position. They were gentlemen who had no wish to force themselves into an intimacy with a cold, sour-faced foreigner, with a wonderful idea of his superiority over them.

The host of the Oak was more curious than my contemporaries, for he seized an opportunity of intercepting me on the landing-place, when I was proceeding to my room, to ask me if I was a friend of Mr. Ehrhardt's.

I replied in the negative.

" I beg pardon," he said in some confusion; " but I saw you coming down the pass together, and I thought that you had been together all day."

"We have been sketching together, certainly."

"Oh! then, you know the gentleman,
sir?"

"I have spoken to him—that is all," I
answered. "Why do you ask?"

"I've no ve—ry particular reason," said
the host, in a hesitative manner. "I've no
complaint to make; only, sir, the truth is, I
fancy that he's a trifle queer in the head.
He's got a bad habit of talking all kinds of
rubbish in his sleep—German rubbish, most
likely, for there's not a bit of sense in anything he says; and he cries and laughs with
it now and then, and that's not pleasant to
hear in the middle of the night, especially
as his room is next to mine, and nothing on
earth will make him change it. I hope that
it is not likely he's going out of his mind,
sir, but I should certainly be more easy in
my own mind if I thought that he had any
friends, or knew anybody, anywhere."

"Yes, I understand;" and then I went

thoughtfully to bed, with Karl Ehrhardt on my mind also.

I met him in the pass next day, at the same spot, and at the same hour, still busy with his picture. I was returning from a long walk when I encountered him, and was surprised to find him rise from his camp-stool to shake hands with me.

"This is fortunate," he said; "I am glad to see you. I was thinking of you, and regretting your absence, when you came along the winding path ahead there. May I ask a favour of you?"

"What favour is it?" I rejoined.

"This picture is a failure, and my hand shakes terribly. I shall never be worthy of the name of painter, despite my love of art, and my incessant application. You are my master—that little rough sketch of yesterday's convinced me at a glance. Will you, Mr. Whitfield, before the sun dips lower, add a tint or two here that I cannot give myself?"

"That will be to spoil your work."

"No, I think not."

"Two hands to one landscape!"

"Yes, yes—I know all that; but this is a dead level of green, and you can give life to it. I am not a fool, or blind to my own faults. There, sir, take my brush, and be of help to me. I am not well to-day, and it will be a friendly action to assist a brother artist."

I could not refuse his request, and, with some doubts as to my own capabilities, I did my best to impart a different tone to a picture that was certainly tame enough, despite all the pains that had been devoted to it. He did not watch me, as I expected, but flung himself full length on the grass, and lay there like a dead man until my voice aroused him.

"Do you think that that is any improvement?" I asked, at last. The sunset glow had left the rock. and the shadows were deepening in the mountain pass.

He sprang to his feet at my inquiry, and looked eagerly over my shoulder at the picture.

"Yes, thank you very heartily; that is the effect which I could not catch, and which your genius has seized. You will rise in your profession, Mr. Whitfield."

"I hope that I may."

"One moment, before you set the brush aside. Could you paint in a cross there?"

"A cross," I echoed.

"It would give a feature to the land-scape, and a foreign air to it. A cross of stone, such as you may have seen abroad and by the wayside—a cross leaning to-wards that narrow path, with a mass of tangled underwood about its base. Like this."

He sketched it rapidly with his pencil on the back of a letter that he took from his pocket, and then passed the letter to me. Marvelling a little at the strangeness of the request, I painted in the cross at the spot which he indicated with his finger, and then the task was done, and it was time to retrace our steps towards the inn.

It was from that day, possibly, that we became friends. I scarcely know how the friendship began, or for what reason. I might have been flattered by his reserve diminishing towards me, and by his singling me out as a man not unworthy of his company. I found him a well-read man, one who had travelled a great deal, knew something of most countries, and could speak of them with the earnestness and eloquence of the enthusiast.

That he was a discontented, almost an unhappy man, I knew before we had reached the inn that night. He was not satisfied with the position that he had attained in his profession; he had hoped to become a great painter, and now he was degenerating to the draughtsman; he was almost jealous of my success at the Academy, and he spoke contemptuously of himself as a magazine man, one whose initials might be known to a few, whose name would be speedily forgotten, and whose place it would be always easy to fill.

"You will be successful, Whitfield," he said to me, "because you are a patient man. You are wedded to your art, and will be faithful to it. There is nothing to distract you from its pursuit, and fill your brain with fancies."

"No; nor in your case, I hope."

"Not now," he answered gloomily.

I was about to change the conversation, seeing how his face had shadowed at some reminiscence, when he added hastily, as though he feared my next question—

"I had my distractions in the past, but I never speak of them. The past, sir, was a cruel one, and is always dead to me."

"I was not going to pain you by alluding to it."

"Thank you," he answered, as he looked gratefully towards me. At the door of the inn he stopped to bid me good night. They were laughing and talking in the coffee-room, and he shuddered as he listened to their happy voices within.

"They are always noisy here, and I am glad to be quit of them. Good-bye."

"Shall I not see you in the morning?"

"You are not likely to see me any more," he replied; "I leave here at an early hour to-morrow."

"Perhaps we shall cross each other's path again before our holidays are over?"

"No, that is not likely. And," he said, after a short pause, "it is not to be wished."

Whether for his sake or mine, he did not condescend to explain, but he bade me good-bye again, expressed a wish even for my success in life, and then went at once to his room.

The next morning, when I arose, the landlord told me that Mr. Ehrhardt had been gone some hours, and he looked as if he was not sorry to be rid of his customer.

Four days afterwards my knapsack was on my back, and I was proceeding on my journey. My sketch-book was full of ideas, and my holidays were drawing to a close. The time was coming once more for work, and I felt that I should not be sorry to welcome it.

I walked twenty-eight miles that day, reaching in the evening a lonely Welsh village, shut in by the hills, and lying so far out of the beaten track of tourists, that my arrival was a matter for wonderment in the minds of the few who were at their doors and windows as I came into the place. This I had resolved upon making my last halting-spot before I struck off across country towards the first Welsh town boasting of its communication by rail with London. I sought this village in quest of character—in the hope of finding a face or two worth sketching, and transferring in due course to my next ambitious painting. I had been told of heads of the true old Welsh type in

the vicinity, and of faces of wondrous beauty
and rare complexion; thanks, said some
people, to the arsenical springs there, the
only water to be obtained in dry seasons of
the year.

There was one small inn in the place, and
no one within it who could speak English
till the landlord came back from market.
From much gesticulation, shaking of the
head, and general air of excitement at my
advent, I could make out that there was no
room for me at the establishment; but I was
tired with my journey, and felt more inclined to doze away the night in the little parlour than to set forth in search of another
habitation. I drank my ale, and took all
the refreshment that the house could afford
me till the landlord came back on his sturdy
Welsh pony, and found that I had made
away with his supper, and was not disposed
to withdraw.

We came to terms at last for the use of
the parlour till the morning, and he ex-

pressed his regret that his one spare room for the use of travellers was occupied by a gentleman who had arrived three days ago, and unfortunately had fallen ill on the day of his arrival.

"Which is an unpleasant thing to do, look you, sir, for when he was first taken ill he spoke nothing but a foreign gibberish, that not a soul of us could make out, and which the doctor was as puzzled at as the best of us."

I thought of Ehrhardt on the instant, whose track I might have followed step by step unconsciously.

"Is he seriously ill?"

"'Deed and I cannot tell you, sir," answered the landlord; "he's been in a swound for the last sixteen hours. The doctor who comes once a day from the other side of the hills to see him, thinks it's his brain, and don't like the job of coming much. He don't see exactly how he's to get his money if the gentleman dies, unless there's enough to pay him in his pocket-book, which, of course, I have not taken the liberty to look into. But it's a sad business."

"I may know this gentleman by sight," I said. "Shall I disturb him much by seeing him ?"

"Oh! no—nothing disturbs him. He sleeps all day, with his eyes open, which scares my wife a little, whose nerves are not of the best. And indeed," he added, with a little shudder himself, "it's an unpleasant way of going to sleep, to say the least of it."

"I will see him at once."

"Thank you, sir; I shall be glad to hear you say that you know him, or his friends. This way."

He took the lighted candle from the table, and led the way up the bare stairs, his heavy walking-boots making the house reverberate as he ascended noisily. I cried "Hush," instinctively, and the landlord turned round, with his broad red face all smiles.

"Bless you, sir, you might fire a cannon off, and not make him notice you. I wish he would wake up a bit, and bring his senses with him. My wife, sir," he added, pausing on the landing-place to give force to this last piece of information, "said she did not like his looks when he stepped into the house; that there was ill luck to us glowering over his shoulder as he came. And sure enough ill luck it is—and queer that man is here."

He tapped his forehead significantly, and I thought of the remark of the landlord at the last inn. If this was Karl Ehrhardt, there were two men of opinion that he was queer in the head.

"This is the room, sir."

My burly guide opened the door, and I followed him into the room, and towards the bedside of the sleeping man.

Yes, it was Ehrhardt, as I had expected —Ehrhardt awfully changed, with a face of ghastly whiteness, like a dead man's, and with his dark eyes preternaturally distended, glaring at something beyond him, or on the watch for something—perhaps for the last glimpse of the destroyer, who might be near him even then, I thought.

He breathed long and regularly, and I took that for a good sign. One thin hand and arm lay outside the bed-clothes, and I felt his pulse, which was strong and regular, if somewhat rapid. I leaned over him, and whispered his name ; a second time I called more loudly in his ear the name of Ehrhardt. But there was no consciousness in the figure lying there, and not a gleam of intelligence came back to the staring eyes.

"Yes, he is very ill," I said.

"You know him, sir ?"

"I met him a few days since at an hotel. His name is Ehrhardt. He is an artist from London, and well-known in London by those who employ him. You need not fear for your expenses, I think."

"Thank you. I am glad to hear you say

that; for we're not rich people, and find it hard to pay our way."

" When will the doctor come again ?"

" To-morrow morning."

" Is this man to be left in the dark till the morning—and with no one to attend upon him ?"

" The daylight comes early," said the land-lord, half apologetically; " and as for a nurse, though the doctor says it doesn't matter much, still we've tried to get one, but they're all afraid of him. They don't like nursing strangers in these parts; and they don't believe he's human altogether. Mrs. Jones says that she thinks he's the devil; but I don't believe," he said gravely, " that we shall ever be lucky enough to see the poor soul so low as that."

" I will sit in this room instead of down-stairs," I said. " Leave me the light, please, and send up my knapsack."

" You're very good, sir; and, as he's a friend of yours, perhaps it's not quite the thing to leave him to himself. If he gets better, he'll take it kindly of you, no doubt; and if he dies, there's the satisfaction of having done one's duty. But, oh! dear, I couldn't sit up with the stranger for the world."

He left the room, to return shortly afterwards with the knapsack, and with a flask of brandy and some water.

"He might be able to take something suddenly, though we have been told not to try, and not to worry him. And now, is there anything else, sir?"

" Nothing else."

" You'll find that arm-chair very comfortable, and there's a desk beyond that recess, if you'd like to write to his friends and make inquiries. He may be in debt, for what we know, sir, or had his money before he'd done his work, as some of you gentlemen do sometimes, I hear."

The landlord, who was evidently a deep thinker, and possessed some knowledge of the world, bade me good night after these various hints, and I was shut in with the stricken man till morning. Ehrhardt had no claim upon my friendship then. We had not exchanged many words together, and he had expressed no wish to renew our acquaintance when we were together in London ; but, had I not felt already an interest in the man, my pity for his condition, lying there so helpless and uncared-for, would have compelled me to impose upon myself the task which I had undertaken. I had no fears—I was not a nervous man— and he was a brother-artist, sick, perhaps, unto death, and surrounded by superstitious or callous people, who cared not if he lived or died, so that he troubled them not.

I trimmed my candle, which was a hideous and malformed thing of tallow—in which my landlady would have doubtless found a winding-sheet or two had she taken the trouble to inspect it—and then I looked round the room and across the bed at

Ehrhardt. He was lying very still, looking far ahead of him, and I wondered where his thoughts were as I gazed at a face that seemed not vacuous to me, but full of an interest beyond the chamber and the present hour. I called him by his name again, but with the same result; I moistened his lips with weak brandy and water, but there was no consciousness in the sufferer. I moved about the room, arranging the place to my liking; I gathered up some sketches from his portfolio, which was open, and put them in their places, fastening up his portfolio again, and laying across it a heavy stick, which could be turned into his camp-stool when necessary. I had felt fatigued before taking my place of nurse, now I was wakeful, and anxious to remain awake. I was restless, and there was a sense of responsibility upon me which I felt would last until the doctor came, or Ehrhardt changed for the better.

When all had been arranged to my taste,

I thought of one hint that the landlord had given me, and which it would be friendly as well as politic to follow—namely, to write to the proprietors of the magazine for which Ehrhardt was engaged as artist, telling them of the illness that had suddenly seized one of their staff, and asking them if there were any friends of his with whom they could communicate in London.

After one more glance at Ehrhardt, I took my candlestick into the recess which had been pointed out to me, and found a desk and writing materials ready to my hand. In the recess also was the picture that Ehrhardt had painted in the mountain pass, and which I had helped him with. He had been intent on fresh alterations lately, and had set up his easel near the great lattice window that was above the writing-desk. I glanced towards the painting, and the change therein struck me on the instant as peculiar. The sky was brighter, and resembled more an Italian sunset than

an English one ; more trees, heavy over-
hanging pines, had been painted in the
background, on the bare slaty hill-side,
which had been, as it were, a foil to the
cleft and the larches, and there was a woman, with long, fair hair, kneeling by the
cross which I had sketched, and praying
there, with her face averted from the gazer.
The whole painting was certainly more a
foreign than a Welsh scene, and I wondered
at the eccentricity which had thus changed
it at the last.

I wrote my letter to the publishers, and
then I began a long epistle to my father,
telling him of my tour and of my last adventure, and how I feared that it was likely
to end.   It was a calm night, and the village
below the window at which I sat was as
still and calm as the night itself.   There
was no wind astir to echo and moan amongst
the mountains, and the stars shone down
upon me through the blindless casement,
and looked very bright and peaceful.

Suddenly, and never, to my poor judgment, to be satisfactorily accounted for, a sense of fear, or of awe, stole over me. For no reason then to be perceived—for I have said that I was not a nervous man, and I had become accustomed to my post as watcher long since—there came an icy feeling to my veins, a sense of coldness and numbness, which I could not resist any more than I could stop the strange thrilling at my heart. I left off writing to listen, and I fancied that the breathing of Ehrhardt was suspended with my own. I thought that he might have died, and I had become conscious on the instant, and as if by instinct, that I sat alone there—that the mighty presence of the dead was before me in that house. I had not the courage to look round; I had become suddenly a coward. I had been sitting with my back to the sick man whilst I wrote, and I could not turn at once, feeling conscious that there had come a change to him since I had seen him last, and that I had been warned of it mysteriously.

All was still, and the Summer night seemed to have grown intensely cold. I struggled with my new fear, and looked round at last.

Ehrhardt was not dead, but sitting up in bed, with one long, bare arm protruding from his shirt-sleeve, and his hand pointing across the room towards a something near the fireplace. The eyes were more distended still, and yet full of a life and eagerness that I had not seen in them before, but the face was ghastly and livid, and was awful to confront.

" Ehrhardt," I cried at last, " what is it?"

He took no heed of my question. His gaze went slowly to the left, away from me, as if following an object round the room, and his finger pointed towards it, and moved slowly with his eyes.

" Marie," he whispered, with a distinctness that startled and chilled me.

To his imagination there was a something which had roused him from his death-like stupor into waking life. Even to mine, in that hour, and under those peculiar circumstances, I could believe that it was there, an unseen but not unfelt presence, brought, by a strange mystery of sympathy existing between the dead and the living, into the room that night. All imagination possibly on both sides, and the heated brain of the sick man affecting by degrees the cooler one of the watcher; but a marvellous coincidence, at least, and still unaccountable in all its intricacies to me. Looking back upon it, there is no solution to the riddle which I accept; the mystery is with me, still perplexing me, though all pertaining to it has long since passed away.

"Ehrhardt," I gasped forth, "this is fancy; you have been dreaming. Pray compose yourself."

He did not heed my words or look towards me. Had his eyes turned once in my direction, I might have believed that my unlooked-for coming had startled him on his return to consciousness; but his gaze was upturned now, as at some one whom he loved, and who might be bending over him.

"Marie," he murmured; and, to my surprise, in Italian, of which I knew a little, "my own Marie, whom I loved so well, you come to me again; not in anger, but with forgiveness for all the cruel past. Tell me so, and save me!"

He leaned more forwards, as if in intercession; there was passion—entreaty in his earnest tones of voice.

"I knew that you would come to-night. I have been waiting for you anxiously. Is it forgiveness at the last?"

He paused as for an answer to his entreaty, and then fell back with a wild cry of "Not yet!" that is ringing in my ears still.

I was at his bedside the instant after-

wards. The feeling of awe which I had had
left me suddenly and completely, and I was
raising his head and trying to induce him to
drink of the stimulant that I held to his lips.
He did not go back to his past immobility,
but after awhile drank from the glass, and
then looked long and steadily at me, as if
puzzled to account for my appearance in his
room.

"How long have you been here?" he
asked, in a faint voice.

"A few hours only," I replied. "I
found you lying ill at this place, and thought
that I would not leave you wholly in strange
hands."

"You are kind."

"You recognize me?"

"Yes; you are Mr. Whitfield, the artist.
Thank you for your sympathy. I was
struck down suddenly, and have been raving,
I suppose. What did I say?"

"Nothing of importance. Will you try
to sleep now?"

"Yes.　I am very weary.　What time is it?"

"Past one."

"Past one of the morning of the twenty-second of July.　So we begin another year, and march onwards with another load."

"Your birthday, Ehrhardt?"

He did not reply for a while, then he said slowly, "I will try to sleep."

He was sleeping calmly the next minute; and I thought what a sorrowful, heart-heavy face it was at which I gazed, and wondered what troubles and temptations the sleeper had passed through in his brief career, to give him that look of unutterable sadness.

He was better the next day; before the week was out he was able to leave his room and walk a little way, leaning on my arm; and at the end of a fortnight he was as strong a man as I had known him first.　He spoke no more of his illness—rather, he shunned the subject as objectionable; but I felt that he was grateful for the interest that

I had shown in him. From that day we were true friends. He was anxious to proceed to London with me, to know my address in London, and to give me his own; to arrange future meetings between us, whereby we might know each other better, and learn to become attached as brothers to each other.

We were of the same profession, and both single men in London. Before the Winter came we were inseparables, and shared the same apartments together.

Despite his many faults, of which a jealous, fretful disposition was not the least, I liked Karl Ehrhardt, and I am sure that he liked me. Sometimes I used to fancy that we had not a secret from each other— that there was implicit confidence between us; and then his strange illness, and his wild cry of Marie, seemed to indicate a trouble which he had not cared to confess. Of women he seldom spoke, if he could help it; and only once, and in a very careless

way, he told me that he had been engaged
to be married, that the lady was too young,
and the match was broken off, which was a
good thing, he added, for her sake as well
as his.

I asked him the lady's name, when this
story oozed out, and he said Francesca; and
then changed the subject, never to allude to
it again.

It was the middle of April, when an
opportunity presented itself for me to see
Italy under favourable circumstances, in the
company of an art-patron—a nobleman and
a gentleman—one who had been the first
to encourage me in my career, the man
reverenced by young artists—the purchaser of the first picture. He wished for a
companion. He was, in his way, an artist
himself, and loved my craft with a true
student's love ; and the offer was too good
and too valuable a one for me to refuse,
had even my wishes lain in a contrary direc-

tion. I accepted his offer, and returned with the good news to Ehrhardt, whose reception of it I shall never forget.

He shouted at me in his jealous fury, and said that I was a fool to become the lackey of any man; that, had I wished to see Italy, he would have thrown up his engagements and accompanied me; that I had not treated him fairly in taking him by surprise, or shown my friendship to him by deciding on my future course without consulting him. He was sorry that he was to lose me for a few months, and took not the most graceful way of showing it; but he calmed down after awhile, and at my sober reasoning with him, and hoped that the journey would be pleasurable and profitable to me.

"You will like Italy," he said; " nay, you may not like any country afterwards, for Italy makes enthusiasts. How long shall you be away?"

"Three months, perhaps."

" You will not be in town till next July, then," he said, thoughtfully.

" About the middle of July, I believe," was my reply.

" Well, I shall miss you very much," he said, with a heavy sigh that pained me to hear, and made me feel as if I had not acted fairly by him ; " but the time will pass away, and presently we shall be together again—I hope," he added, doubtfully.

When the day of my departure came, he was nervous and excitable.

" If I had only the means, the opportunity, the courage to accompany you !" he said.

" Why the courage ?"

" I feel afraid of Italy, it would oppress me too much ; I was never quite myself there."

" When were you there, Karl ?"

"Five years ago next July. What a long, weary time it seems to look back upon !—how impossible to have lived through it all, and be here! There, there —don't mind me and my ravings. Heaven speed you, and good-bye!"

So I parted from my friend, and began my tour in Italy. It was a long and extended tour; my companion loved his ease and took his time. We had not half studied the great country when the Summer was upon us, and it was the time when I had promised to return to Ehrhardt before I was aware. I had corresponded regularly with him, and he with me; he did not press me to return, but bade me take my time and see all that I could under the auspices of my patron. He was well, he said, and doing well.

The first week in July I wrote to him again from a quaint, isolated Italian village, twenty miles or so from one of the great cities. I had met with a singular incident, as it seemed to me, and I sat down to give him the particulars of it at once. The incident was this:—

My companion had been detained in Florence for a few days, and I had journeyed on another stage, and was awaiting his arrival at the village, sketching some of the fairest landmarks of the place whilst I remained there. It was in one of my rambles in a romantic valley that I came upon a scene which struck me as wild and attractive, and yet was not wholly strange to me. For the first few moments I imagined that I had chanced upon a portion of my past route again, the scene seemed so familiar; and then suddenly the jutting piece of rock, the cleft, the pines growing up the mountain-side, and one wild tree standing in fantastic fashion from the rock, with its branches extended like a suppliant's arms for mercy, reminded me of the Welsh scene that I had sketched a year ago, when I had met Ehrhardt in the mountain pass. And yet not resembling so much the scene itself, as the picture which Ehrhardt had made of it, becoming, as I studied it, the landscape in its details, even to the mass of trees in the background, and the old stone cross standing back from the roadway, half choked with the weeds that grew about it. It only required the figure of a fair-haired woman kneeling with her face averted, to give me Ehrhardt's picture—the fair-haired woman whom Ehrhardt might have loved once.

I wrote to him of this discovery of mine, and asked him if I were not right in asserting that this had been his favourite spot in the days gone by, when he had admired the South and lingered in it. This, as part of my news, the conclusion to all the petty details of my journey, and then the inn-keeper waiting for my letter to be sealed, and his man to ride to the city with it.

He was a grave-faced, white-haired old man, who took my letter from me, and glanced at the superscription through his glasses. I was smiling at his curiosity, when he exclaimed—

"Karl Ehrhardt!—that is your friend's

name, then? Ehrhardt, sir, or have my eyes deceived me?"

"That is the name of the gentleman to whom that letter is written, certainly."

"It is strange that I should have come upon it again. I knew," he added, with a heavy sigh, "a gentleman named Ehrhardt once—an artist and a scholar."

"My friend is an artist also, and a scholar."

"Has he ever travelled in Italy?"

"Yes."

"And in this part?"

"I don't know; but I am inclined to think he has."

'But—but this would be very strange. For that Karl Ehrhardt, sir, whom I knew five years ago, ay, and loved like my own son, was a generous and noble-hearted man. He loved some one far beneath him in position and education, but he loved her with all his heart, and would have married her, poor Marie!"

" Marie ! " I ejaculated. " Who was she ? "

" The grand-daughter of the man who has the honour to address you, sir."

" Yes; this is strange," I murmured. " And Marie did not love him. I think I see the story."

" Marie loved him for awhile, but she was very pretty, poor child, and her grand-mother—rest her soul—filled the girl's head with vanity, and so spoiled her for the working world here. I don't know why I should tell you the sad story, sir, only your friend, if it is the same, may tell you a different version, and so do Marie an injustice ; and, alas ! it is no secret in this place. An officer came—an Italian soldier—high-born and proud, who loved Marie too, or said he did, the villain, and then Ehrhardt became jealous, and there were terrible quarrels in this very room. Well, well, the old story of woman's faith and man's deceit. She ran away with him, and broke Karl's heart."

" Marie ran away with the officer ? "

"Ay, that is the story. And yet she loved poor Karl once, for all his odd ways and jealousies, and was grateful to him for his love till the accursed soldier came. She was a beautiful girl, too—more like your English beauties that I have heard so much of, than our dark-haired, dark-eyed Italian girls. I see the gold glistening about her shoulders now, I fancy."

"What has become of her?"

"What becomes of all poor women who act in her fashion, sir? They go away, and are heard of no more by the honest people who loved them, and thought them near the angels once."

"You have not heard of her since?"

"No. She and the tempter both vanished away."

"She may be dead," I said thoughtfully.

"Ah! we should have heard of that, I think. When she is ill or dying, she will think of the old man here, and pray for me to come and see her."

"And her seducer—is there no clue to him?"

"He is abroad, and she is with him, probably."

The man came in to receive the letter from the innkeeper, and he had scarcely ridden away with it, before my conscience smote me for recalling, by my careless lines, a bitter reminiscence to Karl.

"I must have that letter back, if possible. Can the man be overtaken?"

"He has the swiftest mule in the village, sir—it is impossible."

But the effort was made to overtake him, and failed. I wrote a second letter to Ehrhardt, professing to be many miles from the village from which I had dated my first epistle, and feigning an exuberance of spirits which I hoped would deceive him, and assure him that I had learned nothing of that previous history which he had concealed so carefully.

Then I waited for my travelling companion's arrival, which was again delayed; and it was the twenty-second of July when his letter reached me, saying that in the morning he hoped to be free again from all the foreign friends who had made him prisoner. The twenty-second of July: I remembered that it was the night of the twenty-first, and the early morning of the twenty-second when, twelve months ago, I had sat up with Karl Ehrhardt, and thought that he was going to die.

There was angry weather then, and a violent storm, that had raged amongst the hills all day, and had continued after night-fall, was still muttering without the inn, like a thing of evil, that warred against peace and beauty to the last.

The old innkeeper closed his house for the night, and brought me a flask of wine before retiring to his room.

"Have you any further orders?"

"Not any."

"This is a night which I always spend in

prayer," said the old man, "for this is the night on which my Marie stole away. I pray, sir, that she may come back to me in my old age, and find her shelter in these arms from all the scorn of those who are possibly pious," he added drily, "but terribly unpitying."

"On this night she went away, then?"

"Yes, at sunset. The twilight was coming up the valley beyond there when she stole from us for ever."

As he spoke there came across me, for the second and last time in my life, that sense of awe which I had felt twelve months ago—that awful, thrilling, and intense heart-cold against which I had no power to strive. The room was feebly lighted, the lightning flashed blue and ghastly behind the windows. Once I fancied that a figure, and a figure like Ehrhardt's, was looking in upon me, and then I felt that it must be all a dream, and that presently I should wake up in

London, in my little drawing-room, which Ehrhardt shared with me.

But the sense of horror, the consciousness of something near me—at my elbow even—did not leave me, and I spoke as though a voice might be dictating all that it wished me to say, and all that startled me in saying it as at a second self, with different and more cruel thoughts than I had ever had.

"She might have stolen, father, to meet a friend, and found her foe there—she might have died that night."

"Ah! if it had been so, and she dying innocent, poor girl!"

"Ehrhardt might have met her—say in that wild place where the cross is, and in his jealousy and despair, feeling that her love for him was passing away—he might have slain her there, and buried her."

"Great heaven, how dark a thought of yours, sir," cried the old man, clasping his hands together. "What can make you talk like this?"

"He may have been mad," I continued, "and, in his mad reasoning and baffled love, have thought it better to destroy her in her innocence—cut her off suddenly from life—than let her follow the villain who had written for her to come to him, and written words that might be tempting her afresh, when her heart was full of sorrow at his absence. Ehrhardt might have known all this, guessed all this, and argued in this shallow way, until the opportunity came for him to murder her. Old man, this may be near the truth, for all that you and I will ever know."

"Mercy on us, how strange you look! Oh! pray say no more."

I was silent; the spell that had been upon me was broken, and I sat aghast at my own strange arguments. The old innkeeper did not go to his room, but sat down before the empty fireplace, and took his head between his hands, to think or sleep the hours away.

He was sitting thus, and I was brooding

over all that had occurred that day, and on that day twelvemonth, when I was a watcher by a sick man's side, when a heavy knocking sounded without, and voices shouted forth the innkeeper's name.

The old man started to his feet, and went with trembling steps across the room, asking who was there.

" It is I, good Rossi," cried a man from without. " Open the door, please, and then keep back a bit, or the sight may scare you; we bring a dead traveller from the valley."

" A dead traveller!" gasped forth the inn-keeper, as he unfastened the door. "Struck by the lightning, perhaps—poor man !"

" I don't think so, for there's no mark upon him. Beppo says that he saw him in the city this morning, and heard him bar-gaining for a horse to bring him on here. The horse may have thrown him, but he looked more like a man asleep from weari-ness, as he lay at the foot of the old cross, where your poor Marie used to pray."

"Let me see him," I said. Then I went into the tempest in my impatience and new fear, and turned down the cloak from the still, dead face, whilst Rossi held the lamp, and shaded it with his shaking hand.

Yes, it was the face of Ehrhardt, the face of the friend whom I had met in the Welsh glen, from whom I had parted a few months ago, and whose life and death were for ever afterwards parts of the mystery which no power of mine could pierce.

But there are times when I think of him as my friend still, and times when I recoil with the belief that Marie met her death at his hands in the valley where the cross is, and where he had died himself, repentant, begging, perhaps, for that forgiveness for which I had heard him plead once.

TITO'S TROUBLES.

TITO'S TROUBLES.

Y OU are all aware that my first school
was not a fashionable academy for
young gentlemen. Family reverses, not to
mention an exceedingly large family, prevented my father from placing me in a high-
class, high-priced, high-pressure seminary,
when I arrived at that objectionable age
which necessitated my becoming a nuisance
at home to my parents, and to all my little
brothers and sisters. It was absolutely
necessary that I should go somewhere,
everybody said ; and after much hard study
of advertisements in the daily papers, and
personal inspection by my father of half-a-

hundred establishments, I found myself one morning settled at Mr. Price's, Belvoir House, Flatborough-on-the-Sea, an establishment where boys under fourteen years of age were educated, boarded, and generally attended to for the sum of eight-and-twenty pounds per annum. This was not a fashionable price, and it was not, in consequence, a fashionable school. It was, indeed, rather an unfashionable school; the pupils were not highly trained, and were never "civilly examined," and the master had not thought of deposing "quarters" and taking to "terms." There were no extras, there was not a resident mathematical master, and the principal himself taught us all the French he knew, and left the pronunciation a great deal to our tastes.

Still, looking back, I am disposed to think that this was a good school—an old-fashioned school, perhaps, but where the master worked hard in the midst of his boys, crammed no particular clique to the detri-

ment of the rest, and at least did his best—
and he was a clever man in his way—to
give us a sound English education. As a
start in a boy's life, possibly not as a finishing school, Belvoir House was particularly
suitable; and as the situation was healthy,
the terms low, and the master well known
as a man kind to his pupils and interested
in his profession, Mr. Price had always
some sixty or seventy boys beneath his
care.

Mr. Price was not a rich man; indeed
report said that, owing to indiscreet invest-
ments in public companies, he had lost the
little that he had managed to save, before
his own large family—twelve "grown-ups"
sat down to dinner every day of their lives,
and there were four boys under fourteen in
the school itself—prevented him putting
anything more by for a rainy day.

It was at this school that I met Tito
Zalez—and it is Tito's school-life and
strange school-troubles in which I am

about to attempt to interest you. I suppose that I took readily to Tito because he arrived at Belvoir House on the same day as myself, and we both sat in a waiting-room, on chairs much too high to allow of our feet touching the ground, staring sheepishly at one another, whilst our parents were in solemn conclave with the master in the drawing-room. I was eleven years of age, and Tito, I learned afterwards, was ten. I was a thin, gawky, bullet-headed youth for my age; Tito was big and plump, with a dark skin, black curly hair, a nose that young ladies, I believe, call "dubby," and two little bead-like eyes which rolled a great deal in his head, and somewhat alarmed me after my father had shut me in with him.

Our conversation was disconnected and terse. The following was the dialogue that ensued between us, with an interval of about three minutes and a half before either committed himself to a reply.

"What's your name?"

" Joe Simmons.   What's yours?"

" Tito Zalez."

" Oh, is it?"

I thought that it was a very odd name, and that I should not like to have it myself, and that the boys would be very severe upon it presently in the playground, and " chivey " him.   After considering the matter in all its details, I told him the result of my deliberations, and he opened his eyes a little wider with amazement, and said—

" Do you think so, really?"

I said that I really did.

Another long pause, and just as it struck me that he was going to sleep, and likely to pitch off his chair on to the smallest boy's box that I had ever seen, he said,—

" Where do you come from?"

" Reigate."

Of course I asked him where he came from, and he said London.

He was a very curious boy, or else he was anxious to show off that afternoon, and impress me with his importance, knowing that my questions were simply an echo of his own.

"What's your father?" he said.

"He's in a bank. He scoops money out and in—gold money!"

"Lor!"

"What's your father?"

"He's a gentleman."

"Oh!"

I believe this was all the conversation in which we indulged until my father, and Tito's father, and old Price—we always called him old Price, and intended nothing disrespectful thereby—came in to us again. I looked at Tito's father, and was greatly impressed by him at first sight, and though exceedingly flattered by his notice, secretly wished that he would have stared at me a little less. He was a tall, thin man, with a long grey moustache, and with a face very sallow and wrinkled,—so seamed and knotty a face that it reminded me at once of the carved knob

of an eccentric walking-stick which had belonged to my grandfather, and was treasured
by my father for old associations' sake as well
as for its ugliness.

He came to me after he had shaken hands
with Mr. Price.

"You and Tito begin life together," he
said, with a strong foreign accent, "and will
have your way to fight together. Tito is
younger than you, and you must not let the
big boys bounce—I think you boys call it
'bounce'—over him too much. This little
fellow of mine, Master Simmons, has never
been away from home before, and so I leave
you to take care of him."

I believe that I said, "Thank you, sir;"
and after he had shaken hands with me, he
took Tito up in his arms, kissed him once or
twice, and then marched with his head very
erect out of the room, followed, after adieux
had been exchanged, by my father. This
was my first introduction to Belvoir House,
and when Mr. Price had taken a hand of

each, and led us into the playground, the ordeal of the great change was completed, and we were at home before the night had fallen on our new world. I do not know that Tito was quite at home, although he had been lively in the playground, and had laughed a little—and a very fat laugh he had too, which made one laugh to hear it— for when we were in "dormitory six," somebody began crying in the night, and the junior usher, who slept in a large crib in the corner, sat up in bed and asked who was making that noise, but getting no answer save muffled sobs and strange effervescent sounds, as of a youth in the agonies of strangulation, he lighted a candle, and came shivering along the line of iron bedsteads until he found Tito, with his mouth full of sheet and blanket, crying all over his clean pillow-case.

"Now then, Zalez, what's the matter?"

"Oh, please, sir, I wa-a-ant to go ho-o-ome."

"Go home?" said the usher, kindly; "why, you've only just come. Besides, see how cross your father would be after all the trouble he has taken!"

"N-n-no, sir, he would—would-n't. He's too-too-too fo-ond of me."

The usher—Mr. Banstock was his name—sat down and tried to reason with Tito, but with very little effect. He told him that he would soon get used to the change; that he was keeping the other boys awake; that I, Joseph Simmons, from Reigate, was not crying; that Mr. Price would be very cross if he heard him; and that he himself, who was a martyr to rheumatism, would be laid up in the morning if he sat there any longer. But Tito continued to cry, and to make desperate attempts to suffocate himself with the bedding, until Mr. Banstock, as it appeared to me very improperly, promised that he should return home by the first train in the morning.

Tito was calm after that, and stammered

forth, by way of apology for his disorderly outburst, that he knew his papa would be glad to see him back, now that his mother had only just gone away, you know, and left him so much alone, sir!

"Gone away—where?" I heard Mr. Banstock ask.

"Why, to Heaven, sir, papa says."

Mr. Banstock asked no more questions, but went back to his bed, where I heard him tumbling about restlessly, with all the sleep clean out of him, for half an hour afterwards. Once I heard him say, "Poor little chap!" but when I ventured to look over the bedclothes, and say, "Did you speak, sir?" he told me very sharply to hold my tongue, and that if I did not mind he would give me three cube-roots in the morning. I thought that I did not mind, and that I was very much obliged to him; and I went to sleep at last, wondering whether Mr. Banstock would have to get up early and dig his roots out of the garden, and what possible use they would be to me after he had digged them. However, I did not get my cube-roots the next morning, although I found out all about them before the first quarter was over my head, and did not congratulate myself upon the discovery.

Tito and I were firm friends before the first quarter had expired, for he did not go home in the morning, but had a little talk with Mr. Price in the ante-room again, and came out more composed in mind after the master's gentle reasoning, and very red round the eyelids, like a rabbit. Tito, I may add, was a general favourite after his three months' sojourn at Belvoir House: he was a good-tempered, affectionate boy, not particularly clever at his lessons, and getting into difficulties at times concerning them, but taking the ills that academic flesh is heir to with philosophy, and doing better next time, and making up by perseverance for his want of genius. At the end of three months, Colonel Zalez called. We knew by that time that Tito's father was, or had been, a Colonel somewhere, and we felt that he would have greatly obliged the boys of Belvoir House by coming to see his son in full regimentals. I remember that he entered the playground one Saturday afternoon, that Tito suddenly gave a scream of delight, broke a window of the schoolroom with his elbow in his haste to leap down from the sill on which he and I had placed ourselves, and went with a mad plunge at his father's long legs.

Colonel Zalez lifted the boy up in his arms, and kissed him all over his fat face, till some of us certainly burst out laughing; and then he walked up and down the playground for a few minutes, holding Tito's hand, and looking down at him with grave interest. It struck me—it struck two or three of us even—that Colonel Zalez's boots were somewhat down at heel, a fact which was accounted for by young Miles saying that no doubt the Colonel had been marching a good bit lately, which we thought immediately he had. He came to us soon after this discovery, and to my surprise and confusion, and to the infinite amusement of my contemporaries, he stooped down and kissed me, tickling me very much with his bristly grey moustache.

"Tito says that you have been very kind to him, Master Simmons," he said, shaking hands with me after his embrace; "I thank you very much, young gentleman."

I should like to have told him not to mention it, but remained red and silent.

"I have asked permission of Mr. Price to take you and Tito for a stroll this afternoon, and to the circus in the evening, if you would like to go with us."

I found my voice then, and my hearty "Thank you," was very conclusive evidence that I should like to go with them very much indeed.

That was a memorable holiday, eclipsing the holiday last week which I had had with

my father, who had not asked Tito to join
us, as Tito's father had asked me. A holiday marked with a white stone in my calen-
dar of recollections—bright, sunshiny, inef-
faceable—which, described to the boys
afterwards, rendered some of them raving
mad with jealousy, and heaped Tito for the
next three months with attentions that he
could scarcely bear up against, the impression being general that Tito's father had determined to reward munificently all little
Tito's friends. We had buns and almond
cakes at the pastry-cook's, both in our best
clothes; Tito in a new suit of black that his
father had brought with him. We went for
a sail on the great calm sea before the sun
went down; we went back to the pastry-
cook's and had tea, with buns and almond
cakes; we went for a drive in a hired fly before the horsemanship commenced, and
Colonel Zalez lay back and smoked paper
cigarettes so furiously that I thought he
would set himself on fire before the circus

was opened; we went back to the pastry-cook's, and had two bottles of lemonade, and some buns and almond cakes; we attended the performance in the circus and saw wonders upon wonders, and screamed with laughter at the clowns, and thought it was odd—at least I did—that the dark grim face at which we looked when a good joke was uttered, did not change more frequently; we went back to the pastry-cook's to supper, and had buns and almond cakes, and weak sherry and water as a parting stimulant; and finally we were walking on tiptoe through dormitory six—absent-with-leave fellows—looking down compassionately on boys who had been asleep for hours! It was a great holiday; it was the only one that I ever had with Tito. At Christmas, Tito's father came in a hurry to Mr. Price, settled the bill, and then went away again, leaving Tito behind him, after many embraces, and much whispered advice. It began to be understood, after he had departed,

that Tito's father was going abroad—going
to battle, Tito said, very proudly—and that
Tito was to be left at school all through
the Christmas holidays. We bade him
good-bye, and felt very sorry for him, and
my last glimpse of Flatborough-on-the-Sea
that "half" was a curve of the embankment,
a steep green hill, and Tito jumping about
thereon and waving his handkerchief to me.

Next "half" Tito's father did not appear,
and Mr. Price began to look anxious when
Tito spoke of his papa; but at the beginning
of the next quarter, when the Midsummer
holidays were over, a letter came from
abroad that appeared to relieve our master's
mind, and that contained a second epistle,
which Tito used to read to me and to himself, until it became worn out by constant
reference, and by being kept along with his
marbles, a pocket-knife, and a pegtop.

It was an English letter, of course, for
Tito had been born and bred in England,
and had seen no other country; and it was

a very kind, fatherly, humorous kind of epistle, full of hope in his return to England before the next quarter was at an end, and of his anticipation of another holiday with his son and his little friend Simmons, if Simmons were still at Belvoir House. I hoped that he would come back soon, and that a circus would be in the town at the time; but the circus came and went away again, and no Colonel Zalez appeared to keep his promise to us.

"He can't be fighting all this time, Tit," I said in mild remonstrance at Tito's father's behaviour; but Tito shook his head, and said he wasn't so sure of it.

The quarter was past, and the second was approaching its termination. Christmas was upon us again; we were talking evermore of the holidays and home. Tito's father was still absent, and Mr. Price regarded Tito very thoughtfully when the boy said his lessons to him. We went away and left Tito at school—we came back and found Tito there, looking somewhat pale, and his black school suit more than a trifle rusty.

Tito told me confidentially, on my return, that he had received no letter from his father, and that he had heard Mrs. Price say at dinner one day to Mr. Price that she thought it strange, and that Mr. Price had answered that he was inclined to think it rather strange himself, and that he, Tito, was sure that they had been talking about his papa, because they had spoken in whispers, and looked very much at him. I said that it must be fancy, and he tried to agree with me, but hoped that his papa would come to see him soon, for he was out of pocket-money, and his wardrobe was in need of considerable repair. But Colonel Zalez never came, and only Tito his son remained sanguine at last of his return.

I know now, what I did not know in all its details then, that the Prices, *père et mère*, were becoming very anxious concerning the whereabouts of Tito's father—that two quarters were in arrear, that the extra keep during Tito's holiday was added to the account, and that a third quarter had commenced. I knew afterwards that Mr. Price had written to an out-of-the-way place in Central America, where the Colonel had dated his last letter, and that no answer had been returned; that he had written to a British consul and elicited the information that no such person was known within his jurisdiction, and I heard Mr. Price speak once of civil wars and general political confusion, and of the fear that Colonel Zalez had disappeared in a revolutionary vortex for ever.

Lady-day quarter passed, bills were paid, and Tito, waxing shabbier and shabbier, and still wondering why his father never wrote to him, got up every morning with a marvellous confidence in his parent's coming to see him before the day was out. Tito scarcely took into consideration the expense that he was to Mr. Price; he knew nothing of school-bills, and Mr. Price was too tender-hearted a man to show his dissatisfation to the child himself. Mr. Price was puzzled what to do with him, or how long he was to allow this to last, and he looked more thoughtfully at the small enigma every day, and could not see his way to a solution. One day Mr. Price went to London, to the old town address of Colonel Zalez, and made many inquiries at his last lodgings, I learned afterwards, and returned baffled at all points. Tito's father had paid his bill and disappeared about nine months since, without leaving a clue to his whereabouts. A telegram from abroad had led to his sudden departure, it was elicited, and Colonel Zalez, packing up his boxes, and putting on his boots, probably more down at heel than ever, had departed on his mission, whatever it was, to a foreign state, wherever that might be.

Tito became so very shabby after Lady-day that the master found excuses to leave him at home when the boys went out for their airings or their cricket-matches, and finally one of our boys spoke positively to a few high words which he had heard exchanged between Mr. and Mrs. Price one evening, with reference to the former's suggestion that he thought he should risk a suit of clothes for Tito.

The high words at all events ended in the suit of clothes being provided for poor Tito, who accompanied us in our walks again, and looked for the tall, sun-burnt, grey-moustached man at the corner of every street we passed.

Midsummer and the holidays came round, Tito was left at school, and Mr. Price's blank look at the unclaimed one assumed by several degrees more stoniness of aspect. Once more the busy hum of school, old pupils and new ones,—and Tito still on the establishment, and Tito's father nowhere. By degrees the story of the boy's forlorn position had found its way amongst the scholars, and Tito was pitied very much by the majority, and laughed at by a few thoughtless ones, who thought it rare fun for a boy to have a father who had run away from him. Tito's position was not an enviable one, but he bore it pretty well, and only fretted to himself a little, and with not half the noise which he had made on the night when he had missed his father for four hours. I was his counsellor and his comforter, and I kept up his hopes at last by strange legends of various fathers and mothers' returns after years of absence from their children, and was continually ransack- ing story-books for parallel cases to his own.

One day, Mrs. Price and her lord and master began to have a few words again concerning the unfortunate Tito, and Wick- ers, who was the boots of the school by day, and a page radiant in sugar-loaf but- tons at night, came to Tito with the news.

"There's been a jolly row about you,

Master Zalez," he said; "and they've thought it over—only don't you say that I told you, mind—and they think your father is a wenturer, and they're going to send you to the workus."

Tito stared, and finally walked away, keeping from the playground and his play-fellows all day. In the evening he came to me when I was deep in geography, and wrestling with "principal towns," and whispered—

"Joe, I want you."

"What is it, Tit?"

"You heard Wickers say that they were going to send me to the workhouse?"

"Yes—but I don't believe it."

"I'm going to ask the master now—come with me."

"Oh, lor!"

"He's at the desk there looking over the 'Themes,' and I want you to hear what he says."

"Very well."

So I left my place at the imminent risk of getting six bad marks for inattention to my lessons, and went with Tito to Mr. Price's desk. I shall never forget the look of astonishment and discomfiture on the master's face when Tito put the question very straightforwardly, and with wonderful composure.

"If you please, sir, is it true that you are going to send me to the workhouse?"

"Bless my soul!—who—who told you that, Tito?"

"I would rather not say who told me, sir —it's all about the school."

"Dear me—how vexing—how very unfortunate! My poor Tito, I should like to speak to you to-morrow morning, about seven. What are you doing out of your place, Simmons?" he asked, catching sight of me at last.

"I came to take care of Tito, sir."

"Six bad marks."

I knew that I should have them, therefore the promulgation of my sentence did not

take me very much by surprise. Tito might
have made matters worse by getting himself
into a scrape and informing Mr. Price that
he had asked me to leave my place with
him, had not a look from me silenced one
who had quite enough troubles of his own.
Tito went the next morning to Mr. Price's
room, meeting Wickers by the way, who
told him that the master and the missus had
been " at it" again, and that Mrs. Price was
sick of boys whose fathers never paid. Of
the particulars of Tito's conference with Mr.
Price, these are the principal, as detailed to
me by Tito between twelve and two.

It had all been arranged, and Mr. Price
broke the news to him in as gentle a manner
as he could, and wiped his own eyes once or
twice surreptitiously with his pocket-handkerchief. He told Tito that he was not a
rich man, that the school was the support of
himself and a large family, and that it was
beyond his power to keep Tito any longer at
his own expense. He had consulted with

his solicitor, who had advised him to hand over Tito to the parish authorities of Flatborough, who would pass Tito over to the parish authorities of the district in London where Colonel Zalez had resided for many years. He told Tito that the parish would use every exertion, and take far greater pains to find his father than he could do with a great school on his mind, and that he was taking the best and surest means to put Tito in his father's hands once more. He had no doubt that the parish would treat Tito very well, and that Tito would be very happy; but his auditor having his own opinion on this subject, went away discomfited. His last inquiry was—

"When is this to be, Mr. Price?"

"Oh, not this week," said the master assuringly, "or the next. Not till Michaelmas, at any rate."

Somehow the fate that loomed before Tito became known also to the boys, and was canvassed during play-hours, and generally set down as a "jolly shame," not any of us taking into consideration the ways and means of Mr. Price, and the appetite—always a good one—of Tito Zalez, and the rapid growth upwards and sideways—for Tito kept filling out rapidly—of the unfortunate pupil, who was out of his clothes again before any one knew where he was. Once the bright idea occurred to us of getting up a subscription to pay his arrears amongst ourselves and our parents, but the united contributions only amounting, after all the harass of canvassing, to eight shillings and threepence three farthings, it was thought advisable to return the subscriptions to the Tito fund. The second idea was entirely my own, and consisted in suggesting to my father, in a friendly and persuasive note, that Tito would be worth adopting, being a very nice and amiable boy, whom everybody would like at home. This idea was dashed to the ground by my father's courteous but decisive reply in the negative, and Tito, who had built a little on this letter, said "Never mind, Joe," and asked whether Michaelmas-day always fell on the 29th of September.

On the twenty-eighth, in the dusky evening, which steals upon us so early at this date, and when the boys were strolling about the playground, waiting for the bell to ring them to tea, Tito suddenly came to me with the bottoms of his trousers tucked up, and his threadbare jacket buttoned to the chin, in a way that looked like business, and said,

"Good-bye, Joe—I'm off."

"Off!—off where?"

"Hush! don't make a noise; but I can't stand the notion of a workhouse—I'm afraid of it; and—ugh!—the skilley! To-morrow's Michaelmas Day, and I'm going to run away."

"You don't mean it?"

"Yes, I do."

"But what's to become of you?"

"I shall enlist for a drummer, perhaps, or turn farmer's boy, or something. I'm off

at once, through the school window, over
the washhouse tiles, and so into the back
lane."

Tito's sudden resolution took all my breath
away; the novelty of the expedition aroused
my love of adventure, and regardless of con-
sequences, future hardships, future punishment from the hands of Mr. Price, and the
sin of disobedience to my pastor and master,
I said—

"I'll go a little way with you, Tit, and
come back again before they shut up for the
night."

"But how you will catch it!"

"Yes, I know that; but I should not like
you to start alone."

"Thank you, Joe; it's very kind of you:
but I think you had better stop."

I thought so also, but I went with Tito;
and we succeeded in getting from the school
by the way which my small friend had in-
geniously sketched out. When we were
outside the playground wall, and heard the

boys' voices welling to our ears from the other side, our hearts sank a little at the boldness of the step, and we hurried on somewhat crestfallen to the sea-shore, and went on by long low-lying sands, knowing that the tide was out, and that we were not likely to meet anybody at that hour to stop us before we reached the King's Gap. This was a cleft in the cliffs, where I was to part with him, and wish him God speed on his journey. Tito had a bundle with him, in which he had packed a small great-coat, his socks, one shirt, a cricket-ball, a large bag of marbles—the boys were always giving him marbles, by way of token of their respect for him—a few halfpenny prints which he had coloured, and a volume of fairy-tales that his father had given him. The night was soon upon us, and we grew less stout-hearted in the darkness, and were doubtful if the sea might not come up more quickly than we had bargained for, and cut us off from the King's Gap before our tired legs could wade through the deep sand towards it. But we reached the gap in safety, crept past the coast-guard house on the station, and then paused to consider the next step. This was the place of parting; but a look back at the dark country road I had to traverse, and a sudden remembrance of all the horrible stories I had heard of travellers being assassinated in lonely districts, and of children being stripped by gipsies of their clothes, and turned adrift to die of cold, deterred me from returning to Belvoir House till daylight. I said that I would go on with Tito ; and Tito, who had looked dismally in his direction also, said, "Thank you, Joe," and was evidently grateful for my company.

We were both becoming very nervous, but we kept up appearances for awhile. We took the wrong turning, and found ourselves on the edge of the cliff again. We made a short cut across a field to "try back" for the roadway, and lost ourselves completely. We went wandering about meadows and turnip fields in vain efforts to get off farmers' property, and failed. We were frightened almost to death by a white cow that bellowed suddenly over a hedge at us, and Tito dropped his bundle in his hurry, and we had to creep back cautiously for it, but were never able from that night to set eyes upon it again. We were overtaken by the rain— a heavy, steady down-pour, that washed the last atom of courage from our hearts.

"Joe," said Tito suddenly, "I wish I hadn't come."

"So do I," I assented; and then, with our heads very much bent forward, to keep the rain from our faces, and to allow it more easily to find its way down the backs of our necks, we, two foolish miserable hearts, trudged on, doubtful if we were walking over cross-country to London, or back again to Flatborough. When it came to thunder and lightning along with the rain, the climax had arrived, and Tito burst into tears, and wished that he was in his comfortable workhouse, and that I was out of trouble; and then the friendly shelter of an old shed, with the doors off, suddenly coming across our path, we darted into it, and huddled together in one corner, praying for the daylight. How the long night passed we never knew. We went to sleep at last, with our arms round each other's neck, and thought of "the Children in the Wood." We were scared once more by the white cow, who came in with stately tread out of the rain also, and snorted and sniffed about us, and finally lay down across the doorway, barring our egress, and pretending to go to sleep, Tito said that it might take us unawares when we followed its example. We did not know that it was a cow till the morning, our impression being that it was a bull of the very maddest description, and one to be especially wary of, if we set any value on our lives,

Somehow we dozed off to sleep at last, despite our fears; and when we woke again, hearing the hum of voices near us, we found that it was morning, and raining hard still, and that a red-faced man and a rosy-faced girl, with milk-pails, were looking down upon us in intense astonishment.

"Lawks!" the girl said; "what are you a-doing here? What boys are you?" I looked at Tito, and he returned my glance; our spirits were at zero, and it seemed necessary to give in.

"We're from Mr. Price's school at Flatborough, and should be glad to get back," said Tito.

"Flatborough—why, that's fifteen miles from here," said the farmer's man. "You don't mean to say that you two little chaps have been a-playing truant—good gracious!"

But we did mean it; and Tito said that, if they could put his friend Joe in the right road for the school, they might drop himself at the nearest workhouse, when they went that way, as it was all the same, and he was expected there; a piece of information which gave our listeners the impression that we were from the lunatic asylum five miles off. The farmer was sent for, and as he knew Belvoir House well, and was going to Flatborough on business that morning, we were in a fair way towards the end of our adventure, and its unsatisfactory results.

We drove to the school after a breakfast which we were not in a fair condition to enjoy; and Mr. Price, his wife, the assistants, half the boys, and Wickers, were in the hall to see our ignominious return.

"You dreadful boys," Mr. Price said; "what a terrible fright you have given me, and what a deal of trouble! The county police are looking everywhere for you. What made you go away?"

"Please, sir, Tito was afraid of the workhouse," I explained; "and as he did not know his way to London, I thought that I would just put him on his road."

"I'll talk to you presently, Simmons," said Mr. Price, meaningly; and then he turned to Tito and said—"You need not have been afraid of Michaelmas Day, Tito, for I had made up my mind to risk another quarter; but your anxiety of mind was to a certain extent excusable, and I shall not punish you severely."

I felt a twittering all along my spine, but said not a word against his manifest partiality.

"And, my boy, I am very happy to relieve you from a great suspense this morning," said Mr. Price, laying his hand on Tito's curly head. "Here is to-day's paper, with a telegraphic despatch from Central America."

As he unfolded the paper and pointed to one item of intelligence in the top corner of the right-hand column, I bent forwards with Tito, and read, in large letters, the following news concerning a small state, that at this late stage of my story I need not particularly allude to.

"Great Revolution in ——. Release of

Colonel Zalez.   His election as President of the Republic."

Tito's troubles were ended from that day. The next mail brought a letter from President Zalez, whose political intrigues had thrown him into prison, and then had placed him at the head of a government, and Mr. Price's account was settled in due course.

I met President Zalez at an hotel in New York, whither he had gone for a holiday, two years ago, and his son Tito was then a bigger fellow than his father. We laughed over Tito's troubles at a princely banquet which the great man gave us, and, as he smoked his paper cigarettes, we reminded him of our first treat together in the little town of Flatborough-on-the-Sea.

"When you were Tito's best friend," he said, holding out his hand to me across the table. "Thank you, Master Simmons!"

I was afraid that he would have kissed me again in his gratitude, but he sat down, sighed as though the cares of government were a little in the way of the peace and rest that he had found in England, leaned back in his chair, and lighted another cigarette.

AN ODD FIX.

AN ODD FIX.

—

WHEN it came at last to asking Samuel Rowley's consent to pay my addresses to his ward, I knew it was all over with me. I felt that it was all over directly I was shown into the library where Samuel Rowley sat before the fire, toasting his gouty feet, and reading his *Times* newspaper. I felt it was so completely all over with me that I would very gladly have backed myself out of the room, without entering into any particulars as to the object of my visit. I would have cheerfully informed him that I was an agent for Boshiter's Hair-restorer, and had called with a sample, which might be returned if not approved of after one day's rubbing.   But he knew me, and I knew him.   He understood perfectly well why I had solicited the honour of an interview with him at twelve o'clock A.M. ; he was a sharp old gentleman, who had had his eyes on me for some time, and was not to be imposed upon.

He said, "Take a seat, Mr.—I forget your name ;" and then he fumbled with his glasses, and referred to my polite epistle which lay on the table near him.

I took a seat and nursed my hat.   I perspired a little.   I had a tremulous motion of my knees come on, which made me look ridiculous.   I waited for him to begin, but he did not.   I began myself, after one or two secret encounters in my throat with a something which felt very much like a cork out of a soda-water bottle.

"You are not aware—that is, you cannot but be aware—that I have long regarded your ward Clara with—Did you speak, sir ?"

"No, sir, I did not speak."

He had given an awful cough of a double-knock character, that was all. He kept his glasses on his nose, and focussed me, and the operation was unpleasant. He was not pleasant in his reception of my statement either; he was decidedly unpleasant, not to say desperately disagreeable. But then he was a cross, ill-grained old fellow; everybody knew it in Wolverston, and I have no particular reason to disguise it here.

I recommenced my statement; I poured forth the best feelings of my heart, and with an eloquence that might have melted adamant, I confessed to him that Clara was my one ambition. As I have said already, I knew that it was all over with me, but I was poetic even in the midst of my despairing consciousness.

Mr. Rowley set aside his newspaper, drew his chair an inch or two closer to me, put his great hands—rather disposed to be gouty, like his feet—upon his knees, and surveyed me from head to foot contemptuously.

"May I ask your age, young man?" he said.

This was my weak point of defence, but I told him.

"Seventeen."

"And how did you first become acquainted with my Clara, who is a year your junior, the hussy?"

"Well, Mr. Rowley, it has been a long attachment; my finishing school at Beesborough was situated opposite her finishing school, and we saw each other at church; and I think——"

"I think that you both ought to be horse-whipped!" he said fiercely, interrupting me; "and as for my consent to Clara's engagement to a boy like you—I will even go so far as to say a whipper-snapper like you——"

"A whipper-snapper, sir!"

"I repeat it, a whipper-snapper!" cried

old Rowley, becoming very red and apoplectic in appearance. "I decline to listen to your preposterous proposal for one instant. Clara is only sixteen, and does not know her own mind—she is a mere child."

"But we shall both grow older, Mr. Rowley."

"Ah, and more sensible, I hope. Good morning."

"Good morning, sir."

I did not wait to tell him of my expectations from my grandmother, or to reason with him on his want of justice and consideration. I went away crestfallen and heart-broken. I dashed from the library in despair, and brought my forehead against that of my beloved with a concussion that was nearly the means of stretching our senseless forms outside the tyrant's den, the victims of his cruel obduracy. Clara, naturally interested in the result of my interview with her guardian, had forced her pure but anxious soul to listen at the library keyhole. I had retired in haste and floored her.

"Oh, my gracious!" she sobbed forth, "I did not know you were coming out like that! Oh, my head!—oh, how dreadful! Oh, Alphonse, we must part for ever!"

She rested her head on my shoulder and shed many tears. I kissed away her tears; I patted her head fondly, keeping clear of the bumps which I had raised there. I could scarcely see her golden hair for tears myself—the water had risen into my eyes immediately we had met each other. I sought to calm her emotion. I bade her be firm, and I recommended vinegar and brown paper for her damaged brow. I said that I should try them myself when I got home. I told her that I would die rather than relinquish her; she said the same thing in a burst of uncontrollable emotion; we renewed our vows of eternal fidelity, and tore ourselves from each other's arms, crushed in

spirit, but strong yet to resist unjust oppres-
sion.

I told all my troubles to Jack Edwards,
my bosom friend and adviser. Jack and I
had been schoolfellows together; we were
going into the medical profession together
presently: my father had resolved that I
should walk the hospitals instead of the rosy
path of love. Jack heard my story, and
said that he would not have stood half of
old Rowley's nonsense; but what he would
have done under the circumstances he did
not impart to me at the time, and I forgot
to ask him afterwards.

Clara and I met clandestinely. We were
lovers—we had been lovers from our youth
—the flinty heart of a guardian who had
outlived mortal passion was not to stand
between our fresh young souls.

I met Clara in the village; I scaled the
park-fence and met her in the green wood;
and Jack, good fellow, kept watch on the
door of the Hall, and old Rowley's library-

windows, with a telescope, lest we should be surprised at any moment. Clara and I passed much of our time talking of what we would do when she came into her property at twenty-one, and my grandmother favoured me by departing from this earthly sphere; but it was a sharp Winter, and our teeth chattered over our prospects. Clara and I used to arrange our meetings in this wise: Clara had a confidant in the game-keeper, Peter Stokes, an invaluable man, with a weakness for tobacco, and with a heart all charity towards his fellow-creatures. Peter was always getting up subscriptions for his fellow-creatures in the village; and what with his subscriptions and his tobacco—I kept him entirely in tobacco—my pocket-money knew but little rest. Still, he had a good heart, and was kind to us. He took charge of our correspondence, which was carried on by a circumlocutory but sure process. Clara gave it to her maid Selina, another *confidante*—who, alas! proved herself a perfidious snake—and Selina intrusted it to Peter, who took it to a gnarled monarch of the forest—an oak-tree, in fact—and concealed it from all human gaze in a small hollow cavity some ten feet from the ground, where, at a later hour, I found it, and deposited my answer, to be conveyed by the same process into my dearest Clara's hands.

Peter was a lank old man, and very wiry; he could climb a tree like a squirrel, and I was agile myself. The whole conception was romantic, if you will, but grand! I thought so—Clara thoughtso—Peter thought so. The idea was from Millais's picture, which we had both carefully studied; and and if Peter had not generally deposited his small notes to myself at the same time, asking my "kind considerashun, as a gentleman born with a warm hart, to an aflicting kase in the parissh," the romance would have been pure and unalloyed.

Clara defied the obdurate guardian for

two months; it was in February when Selina Muggins betrayed us. I was advancing in an innocent and unsuspecting manner to the secret post-office in the wood, half a mile from Mr. Rowley's house, when I became conscious of the whole perfidy. I was close upon the tree—that brave old oak which had held so many secrets—when voices in another direction filled my soul with horror. They were the voices of Samuel Rowley, Esq., J.P., and Peter Stokes, my Mercury. I sank down in the long grass—there was a rapid thaw that morning, and the damp struck to me at once—and trembled for my love. I was not an instant too soon; their footsteps were upon me. Mr. Rowley's right foot was nearly upon me also; he shaved my features by a hair's breadth, and passed on. The harsh tones of his voice rang in my ears an instant afterwards.

"You don't consider yourself an abominable scamp, I suppose," Mr. Rowley said— " an unprincipled old vagabond, to act as a go-between to a silly schoolgirl and that idiot of a boy! You never thought of the harm of encouraging this, did you?"

" I'm werry sorry, sir," whimpered Peter.

"Teaching my ward to be deceitful, for the sake of a few sixpences, I suppose."

" I've never had a ha'penny, your honour, much more a sixpence."

Neither had he. They were generally half-crowns he was in the habit of receiving from me.

"You deserve to be kicked out of my service, Stokes—drummed out of the village, for a wicked old hypocrite!"

" They were werry fond of each other, sir, and Miss Clara used to ask me so beseechingly; and when I told her there was harm in writing to Master Huskisson without her dear gardewan's knowing anythink about it, she allers said it was for the last time, sir—really."

" If it were not for your age, Stokes, I'd send you about your business this very day."

" I'm werry sorry, sir," Stokes said again, shedding many tears.

" Is this the tree ?"

" Yes, sir, that's the tree."

" And Clara s last letter is up there now, eh ? In that hole? Now, no more lies !"

" Yes, sir, in that hole."

" How on earth do you get at it ?"

" Master Huskisson climbs up there, sir, for his answers. I'll go up and fetch down Miss Clara's letter in a minit."

There was a small epistle of his own he wished to obtain as well, perhaps, or it was possible that his noble mind had suggested some scheme to save dear Clara's missive from sacrilegious eyes. But Mr. Rowley suspected this old servitor.

" Stop where you are, Stokes !" he roared forth ; " I'll have no more of your monkey tricks. Give me a back."

" Give you a wot, sir ?"

" Bend your back, you rascal, and I'll jump on it, and get the letter myself."

"Jump on it!" repeated Stokes, with a look of dismay at Mr. Rowley's portly figure; "it don't strike me that I can bear your weight, master."

"It will be only for a minute," said Mr. Rowley, quite brutally; "and if I break your back, it will serve you right enough. I'm not an elephant, man, and I'll have no more of this nonsense."

Mr. Stokes resisted no farther. He made his back, as if about to commence a game at leap-frog with a justice of the peace; and with more agility than I had given Mr. Rowley credit for, the guardian was aloft, and within an inch or two of our letter-box.

"Oh! lor, shall you be long, sir?" asked Mr. Stokes, groaning softly to himself.

"Raise your shoulder, you rascal, a little more," cried his employer.

Stokes did so, and from my hiding-place I saw the hand of Mr. Rowley strive, with some difficulty—for it was a fat, gouty hand, I have already said—to force itself into that casket, which had contained so many of my dear Clara's epistles. Samuel Rowley was an excitable man; for he swore a little in his efforts, and turned very red and moved his feet restlessly upon poor Stokes's back.

"I have got it!" he cried at last. "The artful jade!—the cunning, plotting little minx, to serve her own guardian in this— Oh!"

"What's the matter, sir?"

"Wait a moment, Stokes—don't shake. Oh! lor, have mercy upon us! Oh! damn it! Oh! dear what is to be done?"

"Is anythink partickler the matter, sir? Not a hadder, I hope, or a nest of sarpents or anythink?" and old Stokes hid his head a little more—tucked-in his tuppenny we called it at school—to conceal his laughing and sardonic countenance.

"No, Stokes; it's something much worse, I'm sorry to say."

"Wus, sir?" said Stokes, who left off laughing immediately.

" Yes. I—I can't get my hand out."

" The devil you can't, sir !" cried Stokes in dismay.

" It's twisted somehow, or swollen, or the wood has gripped me. Wait a moment, Stokes—oh ! it's all up with me ! I can't !"

" Take it quiet, sir. Keep cool, or you'll never do it—don't hagitate yourself—but for God's sake look sharp ! I'm a cracking !"

" Don't move, Stokes—as you are a man, don't move ! If you were to drop, I cannot imagine what would become of me. It will be all right in a minute."

" Make it less if you can," groaned Stokes ; " all the blood's got into my head, orful ! Oh ! lor, what is to be done ? Are you out, sir ?"

" No, I'm not; I'm fixed, Stokes. I'm a dead man, if you move—I am indeed."

Stokes burst into tears, and howled with all his might; and Mr. Rowley shouted a great deal, and swore a great deal too. Stokes would have run for it probably, for he was succumbing fast to the dead-weight above him, had not Mr. Rowley held him by the throat with his boots, and fixed him too. In another moment I had sprung to my feet, and was rushing to the rescue.

" I'm really very sorry, Mr. Rowley ; can I be of any assistance ?"

" Assistance, you—you—young dev—! Yes, you can, my dear child. Run for a ladder, and a saw, or something, as quick as lightning, to the house."

"Hi—hi—hollo!" shrieked Stokes, as I prepared to obey Mr. Rowley's commands ; " don't run—come here, and let me run, or bust up I must! O lor, Master Huskisson, don't leave me any longer—do come and take a turn ! He's not so heavy when you're used to him—he isn't, indeed !"

I saw the necessity of advancing to the rescue at once, and so did Mr. Rowley. I was tall for my age and tolerably strong, and I hastened to take the place of Mr. Stokes, which I did with great caution on all sides. Behold me at last bearing the guardian of Clara on my shoulders, and feeling terribly the weight of my responsibility as he stood with his face to the tree, still exercising his ingenuity to get his hand out of the trap.

"I hope I'm not too heavy for you, Master Huskisson," he condescended to say politely, for the sight of me was even pleasant to witness.

"Not at all," was my cheerful answer. "You'll make yourself as light as you can to oblige me, perhaps?"

I had not quite done growing, and man is fragile during that process. Mr. Rowley was very heavy, and Stokes was wrong in his assertion—wickedly wrong.

"This is all your fault, mind you, Huskisson. This might have been my death," he said reproachfully.

"Yes, Mr. Rowley, if I hadn't been in the way," was my happy rejoinder.

"Ah! but"—he looked round with difficulty, and found Stokes still there, making every human effort to straighten his back before flying on his mission. "Curse it, Stokes, run for your life!—don't stand there, you wretched lunatic, another instant!"

Stokes ran away, and I was left as the one support of Mr. Rowley. Stokes had not been gone more than a minute and a half, when I wished that he had remained and shared the weight with me. I tried to keep firm, but the difficulty was immense.

"Boy, you're giving! Don't shake so. Keep yourself more against the tree," Mr. Rowley called down.

"All right. I'll do it for Clara's sake, if it's possible; but if I snap——"

Then I remembered that he had called me a whipper-snapper; and so did he too, I think, and was sorry.

"Oh, you'll keep up," he said, offering me every encouragement in his power. "You're a big boy for seventeen, and I'm only nine stone ten—not a great weight. I've seen people in a circus do this kind of thing for hours, you know."

It was a gross exaggeration, and I felt it to be one. I was getting faint also. I had undertaken too much; and his language at times was still violent, as he endeavoured to extricate his hand.

"If I should die, sir," I said, feebly, "will you please give my love to Clara? Tell her I did all I could to bear up—and to bear you up. O dear! did you say nine stone ten?"

"I did."

"I should have thought you had been ninety," I murmured.

"You're giving!" he roared again with a vehemence that revived me. "Keep up a little longer, my dear boy. I can hear them coming in the distance."

Which was another falsehood; but no matter. Mr. Rowley was not a truthful man. I set myself firmly against the tree, according to his instructions, but it was of no avail. My heels, in a few more minutes, would slide gracefully away from me, I was certain, and the guardian of my Clara would be swinging about by one arm, like an early Christian martyr. His blood would be on my head, and so would he, if he came down with his whole weight—perhaps armless—on the top of me.

"Keep up!" he cried in a great fright now. "You shall see Clara when you like, my boy. I will not say a word against the match any more. You're a fine, strapping, brave fellow, that you are—a young Hercules!"

"Thank you, Mr. Rowley," I answered; and his words did sustain me a little, and helped me to sustain him.

But I was sliding, slowly but surely, from under his feet, when assistance arrived : men with ladders, and saws, and chisels; and Clara too, wild with fright, and with tears streaming down her cheeks.

"Oh, my poor gardy!" she cried.—"Oh, you wicked Alphonse! it's all your dreadful fault."

This was the last feather on the camel's back. I fell forwards, and a grand rush of the servants at Mr. Rowley's legs only saved the guardian from summary dislocation on the spot. He was got down with difficulty; and once down, he was not grateful.

"A pretty fool you have made of me," he said to Clara, as he walked away rubbing his wrist; "and a pretty pair of fools you and that boy are too!"

Still, after all, he was not so bad as I had expected to find him. He was a man who kept his word, and for that I have always respected old Rowley. Clara and I saw each other in a more rational manner. I went to the Hall once or twice; she was at my house on my eighteenth birthday, at a little party which my mamma absurdly called "juvenile" in the invitations; and there Jack Edwards was too attentive to

Clara, and raised a jealous demon in my breast.

I went to London shortly afterwards. Clara and I were to be engaged when I "passed," and if we were of the same mind, her guardian said. But we were not. Whilst I was walking the hospitals a fellow in the tallow-trade walked off with Clara, and I do not think she resisted in the least.

It was an excellent match, though he was forty-seven, and very stout. I went down to the wedding, and returned thanks at the breakfast for the bridesmaids, one of whom has promised to be *mine* when I set up in business for myself.

NANTLE FERRY.

NANTLE FERRY.

I WAS a younger man by five and twenty years when the strange incidents occurred that form the subject of this story. Twenty-five years ago, and yet not so far away in the past to one who has lived a bachelor's life, and has few landmarks to look back upon. Whether my fault or anothers, matters not. The courting days, if I ever had any, are a misty retrospect, and the shadows that belong to them I will not trouble now.

Twenty-five years ago I was travelling for my health's sake in the North of England. I had been recommended change ;

too much study, or too much trouble, no matter which, had brought me low, and absence from my duties was imperative. The journey was one of the most miserable I had ever undertaken ; the season was bad, my spirits were worse, and I was without a companion in one of the dreariest parts of England. I had started on my tour without giving notice of my intentions to the few friends I possessed in those times. I felt that I should be bad company for any one whose kindness might have prompted him to join me, and I went on my way alone, walking my thirty miles a day, as dismal a figure in an Autumn landscape as it is possible for my listeners to imagine.

The night that begins my story was a cold and dark one in the middle of October. A cold, windy night, with few stars shining out, and no moon due till the early morning. I had walked five and twenty miles that day, and had three more to accomplish before the little village of Nantle could be reached. There was an ugly pass by a dark hillside to travel, and a ferry over Nantle river to be made before the day's journey was ended, and I could escape the cutting north-east wind and the showers of dead leaves it rained upon me and whirled before me on my road. When the Nantle stream was reached at last, and there was no sign of ferryboat or ferryman, I began to wish that I had finished my day's tramp at the inn I had left behind two hours ago. They had told me there, it would be a long and tedious journey, and I had shrugged my shoulders at their prophecy, and marched off manfully. I was seeking " a long and tedious journey " —fatigue and exhaustion were good friends to me, for they helped me to sleep and forgetfulness. Still I thought regretfully of the homely inn I had left behind, of the great wood fire burning on the hearth, and the bronzed, good-tempered face of the landlord as he said, " It was ower late for travellers not well up in the roads," when I was standing at the water's edge, shouting, "Ferry, ho!" and obtaining no response, save a faint "Ferry, ho!" from the distant hills, that caught up my words and mocked me. Once before in my life I had travelled the same road and crossed the Nantle ferry; I knew I was not mistaken in the place, though my late host had assured me that Wisford the ferryman was always at his post, till the hope of a penny was entirely lost him.

"He's as miserly as he's cunning, you must know," was the observation made to me at an early hour of that night. "I've known him as late as midnight at the ferry hankering arter customers that never come. It pleases the old man to turn a penny when honest folk be sleeping. Some say he carries over queer company at times—poachers, ghosts, boggles; he's not particular if he gets his money. Still, if he bean't handy, sing out 'Ferry, ho!' and he'll turn out of his crazy old hut on the t'other side of the river, as joyfully as if you had brought a fortune to him."

The host had prophesied but ill, however, for there I was, shouting at the water's edge, with my hopes of the ferryman's appearance growing fainter every instant. I was debating how to proceed, after the echoes, roused by my last call, had died away; looking with no little dissatisfaction to the long backward road, and with less to fording or swimming to the opposite side, and running on cold and wet to Nantle, when a harsh whisper in my ear made me start, and set my heart for a moment beating rapidly.

" Do you think to wake the dead, sir?"

I had always had some pride in my self-possession; but it was shaken then, I confessed, with some little mortification to myself. Still, a moment afterwards, I was outwardly calm and composed, and stood on the river bank quietly regarding my questioner. A woman, whose age was difficult to determine at that place and at so late an hour; a poor woman, probably, with a shawl of slight material drawn tightly round her, a shapeless bonnet, stuck anyways on her head, and one lock of hair straggling from beneath in a maniacal manner that suggested the first witch in *Macbeth*. A yard or two from her was a great furze-brush, behind which she had probably been sleeping or hiding when my voice aroused her. She could not have been walking lately, or I should have heard her footfall on the loose, stony road I had recently traversed; and I had no faith in supernatural appearances.

"No," I said, in answer to her inquiry; "but I hope to wake the ferryman, my good woman, before I catch cold standing here."

"I don't think the man's alive that will ferry you across the river to-night."

"Do you think the boatman's dead, then?"

"Yes," with a strong shudder, that I could detect in the darkness.

"May I ask if you have any reason for that supposition?"

"I have been waiting here an hour for him, and he has made no sign. A long hour, and the river whispering such awful things!"

I glanced towards the woman again. She was standing with her hands clasped, looking down at the dark water. The wildness of the woman's manner prepared me for any danger, steeled my nerves to resist also her eccentricity, and made me ready to spring at her, should she meditate a leap towards the river from the bank on which she stood.

"Do you believe in calls?" she asked, after a moment's silence.

"Well, my faith is shaken, now I'm getting hoarse."

It was uphill work to strive for a light turn to the dialogue; but the woman's manner was melodramatic, and of melodramatic people I have ever had a horror.

"I mean, calls from the dying to some one loved, or near, or dear. Calls in the last moment, perhaps! You are a scholar, and may have read of them."

"I may have read of some peculiar coincidence of the kind, that might be put down to a call by any one of a superstitious turn of mind. What of it?"

"Nothing," said the woman, moodily.

"If the ferryman has been calling, my good woman, I think it must have been in the flesh, whilst you were dozing here, for there is a light in the window of the hut yonder, and I take it for a sign that I am heard."

"Thank God, then!" said the woman, looking in the direction indicated; where, surely enough, a faint light had suddenly appeared.

"Is that the usual signal to late travellers?" I inquired.

"I believe so. I am a stranger here,"

was the answer, in a changed, almost sullen tone of voice.

"That is the ferryman's hut across the river?"

"Most likely."

I doubted her ignorance, though I kept silent on the point, and intruded no further conversation on my strange companion, who stood watching the distant light with great intentness. I was interested in that light also, for it argued a safe transit to Nantle, and I had nearly given up the hope of it. I called once more, and, whilst the hills were muttering my words, the light was moved a little to the left, as if along a window-sill.

"Good news. The ferryman is waking up."

No notice was taken of this assertion; my strange companion evinced no satisfaction at the prospect of a fair end to her journey. I was speculating as to the object of that visit, and wondering if any superstitious feeling had really brought her at so late an hour on the same road as myself, when the distant dip of oars in the water assured me that the ferryman was still in the flesh, and had an eye to business. Pleased at this promised termination to my adventure, I lighted my cigar, and stood smoking it on the bank, whilst the dark outline of the boat gradually became more evident. In a few moments the ferryman was a couple of boats' length from our side of the river, at which distance he ceased rowing, and stood up in the boat, with a lantern in his hand.

"How many are there of you on the bank? Come more into the light."

"Two," I answered, stepping forward as directed. The woman did not move; but he turned the lantern full on her, and she seemed to flinch a little.

"Both strangers," he said, in a somewhat suspicious tone. "Do you know anyone in Nantle?"

The woman gave a name that appeared to satisfy the suspicious ferryman, whose cross-questioning was becoming trying to my self-possession. However, there was no help for it but civility, if I wished to be ferried to Nantle that night, therefore I briefly responded that I was a tourist, and making for the "Lion Inn."

"The 'Lion's' full," replied the man, "there are people about the railway. You'll get no accommodation to-night."

"A seat by the fire will be sufficient for me."

"It's only seven miles to Berksham."

"I have just left there. Bring your boat nearer, my good man; it's cold work standing here."

"Maybe, maybe; but it's an unco time of night to cross the ferry—waking honest men out of their first sleep. There's moighty talk of queer customers about, though I'm a poor man that it would na' be profitable to harm."

"Will you ferry me across, or not?" I demanded, losing patience.

"To be sure. You're a gentleman, who'll

make it worth my while, I know. I'm very old and poor, and my nerves won't get over this shake up for a month. Now then, sir."

The boat shot towards the bank, and the keel grated against the pebbly bottom of the river. As the woman stepped into the boat he held the lantern towards her again, and tried to peer into her face as she passed to a seat in the stern, the tattered fringe of her shawl hiding her face from view, as she kept one large, ungloved hand pressed tightly to her forehead.

"Tired, mayhap?" he asked.

"Tired to death!" was the reply.

"Death's an ugly word at such a time as this—in such a place too," grumbled the ferryman, as though the observation had been an insult directed to himself.

"Why, at such a time—or in such a place?" I said, as I followed the woman into the boat, and felt the glare of the lantern on my face again.

"Don't ask me—it's a hard story, and I woan't dwell on it," was the reply. "It's a story that's no business of yours, sir."

"Possibly not."

"They will tell it you at the 'Lion' for a mug of ale. You'll know, then, why Jacob Wisford don' care for such a tale. Weugh! how late and cold for an old man to be abroad! Gentlefolks should make it worth his while. I'm seventy-seven come November next."

Having obliged me with this very significant hint, the old man relapsed into silence, and rowed us slowly across the river, keeping his small keen eyes upon me and the woman, as though still distrustful of his company. When we were landed on the other side, and the woman had thrust something into his hand, and hurried away down a narrow lane, at the side of the hut from which he had signalled us a few moments since, he said—

"Who be she, sir, may I ask?"

" I don't know. I found her waiting at the ferry."

" No friend of yours, then ?"

" Oh, no !"

"She's a sight more liberal than I expected from the look of her," said he, stooping and critically inspecting the sixpence in his hand. "She feels for the poor, whose lot is hardly cast. Ah! mayhap she's got a father herself. The Lord be good to you, sir—you're very koind."

I could see the old man's eyes sparkle at the sight of the half-crown which I had tendered him, and the blessing that rewarded my liberality came freely from his heart.

" Real gentlefolks know how to behave to us hard workers. God bless you, sir, for remembering old Wisford ! Straight down the lane to the ' Lion,' sir; the only inn in the place, and that's chock full !"

He gave rather a malicious chuckle at this, which he attempted to smother by a sigh and a shake of the head over the strange faces that were making Nantle anything but what it used to be.

"There'll be a good fire, though," said he, rubbing one hand over the other, and shivering; "and that's more than I could offer you, or afford, at this old house of moine. Cold it be at this time of year. You don't happen to have," he added, wistfully regarding my cigar, "a bit of tobacco or the end of a cigar about you, for a poor fellow who loikes his pipe in noights like this?"

I tendered him a cigar from my case, and received another hearty blessing in return, accompanied by the extra attention of showing me a little beaten track across the green to the lane, by the assistance of his lantern.

"You live there all alone?" I asked, pointing to the hut at the water's edge.

"Yes, lonely quarters they be, sir; but there's no soul to harm me, for there's nothing to be got by it."

"No family?"

"No, no, nothing! Wife, darter, grand-child gone dead, sir, years agone. Good night to your honour. Do you see the track?"

"All right. Good night."

He echoed my good night again, and before I had gone many steps down the lane I could hear sundry bolts being shot within the hut, and the rattle rattle of a heavy chain drawn across the door.

"A careful old gentleman," I soliloquized, as I made the best of my way to the "Lion Inn" at Nantle. The "Lion Inn" was the first house in the village, and not more than three hundred yards from the wretched domicile of Jacob Wisford. It was a small inn enough; but it looked a grateful shelter from the dark, lowering night, as I turned the curve of the lane, and saw the bright red fire shining through the upper panes of a window, only half masked by the low wooden shutter before it. The host of the "Lion," a thin, lank-haired, long man, responded to my summons at the door.

"Fortun' says I ain't to have no sleep to-night," said he, admitting me; "there never was such times at Nantle. Good evening to you, sir. I fear there's little space at your service. Some gents are down here surveying and meas'ring about, and haven't left much room."

"No matter. An arm-chair and my travelling cloak will serve on an emergency."

"You're very kind, sir; but it needn't be so bad as that. We've a spare room up-stairs—sweet and clean, at any rate."

A sight of the spare room, shown me by the host's flaring candle, put me so much in mind of the coffin of a stout uncle of mine, whose funeral I had attended a few months before, that I beat a hasty retreat down-stairs, saying that I would prefer the fireside and the arm-chair.

"You'll have company there, sir—male and female. There is myself, who is sitting up to-night for a gent who is expected late, and there's a poor woman, who came in a minute or two before yourself, that I hadn't the heart to turn away, though it's blessed little I shall get by her. This way, sir."

Into the bar-parlour, or tap-room, or whatever else the host of the " Lion " might choose to designate it, I followed my guide. It was a triangular-shaped room, with a sanded floor and three dark-stained tables, on one of which rested the head and outstretched arms of the woman who had crossed the ferry with me. The bonnet she had worn was lying on at her feet, and her hair—it had been raven black once, but was now thickly sown with grey—hung tangled and disordered over her outspread arms. It was the wreck of a woman—a wreck, perhaps, of all that had been good, and loving, and tender in the maidenhood of years ago.

" Dead beat," said the landlord, sententiously.

" Poor woman! Do you know her?"

" Never saw her afore. Working her way to Pendlehant, she tells me."

" Indeed !"

I composed myself in the arm-chair before the fire, and the landlord took a seat opposite me, and smoked his pipe, and looked reflectively at the flames. Although I was tired, and had made up my mind to sleep, fate was against me that night. Little chance incidents occurred that set my eyes staring widely, just as they were becoming heavy, and I was losing consciousness of outward things. The landlord had a strong, hollow cough, that burst out unexpectedly at times; the woman at the table by the window was restless, and moved once or twice in her sleep; the coals were small in the grate, and would tumble suddenly through the bars to the hearth; and the American clock over the mantelpiece struck one like a death-knell. I gave up the attempt to sleep at last, and regarded my landlord opposite, who still smoked his pipe composedly. When my host was perfectly assured of my wakefulness, he said—

"Did you cross Nantle Ferry to-night, sir?"

"Yes, after some trouble to rouse the ferryman."

"Ah! he's a queer one," observed my host. "I'd lay a wager he was watching you through his night-glass long before he made up his mind to ferry you across. Few more careful people in the world than old Jacob, I take it."

"It struck me that he was a little suspicious."

"He suspects everything and everybody, sir. He don't believe in anything. He's what you larned people call a skipstic. When he comes to the "Lion," sir, he drives me wild with his doubts of a fair pint of beer, or his right change out of it. And he likes his screws of baccer rather larger than anybody else's."

" The way of the world, friend.'"

" Well, it's an uncomfortable way, and aggravating, The more so to me, because I knew him twenty years ago, and he warn't the miserly old hunks he is at present. There warn't once a better man than Jacob Wisford, this side of the Nantle."

" May I ask what misfortune changed his character so much."

I had met with misfortune myself, and was interested in a fellow-sufferer. I was curious to know what had changed the old man's life and character, and whether some lesson might be taught me on my own dark way.

" A hard misfortune, certainly. Twenty years ago he was a widower, with an on'y darter—a darter very beautiful, and much looked upon and liked. It's a story old as the hills, sir—she went wrong."

" Poor girl !"

" Tempted out of her station, sir, by some artist-gentleman who took it into his head to sketch hereabouts at that time, and who met and spoke with her, and wound round her heart like a sarpent—the Lord forgive the villain! He went away, sir, to make arrangements for his marriage with Jenny Wisford, *she* supposed, and time went on, and the old man woke suddenly to the knowledge of the shame his daughter had brought upon his head and hers. He was a good old man, and bore it well. It warn't the sight of his darter's little baby that turned him hard as iron. He grew to love that baby, sir, and to hope in his darter's repentance, and brought her to Nantle Church every Sunday arternoon, to look them down who sneered at her, and thought themselves so precious good. Well, sir, there was worse to come—what's that?"

The landlord of the "Lion" and myself both turned and looked toward the table where the woman slept; but the figure was motionless, and in the same despairing attitude.

The woman had moved again in her sleep—
that was all.

"The worst was, sir, that there came a
letter to the girl one day from London, that
seemed to change her all at once, and make
her hard and reckless. For two days no
one could make her out, she was so wild
and strange ; and then, one night, sir,"
sinking his voice to a whisper, "just such a
night as this, she got up when her father
was asleep, stole out with her child in the
darkness, ferried herself across the river,
sent the boat adrift, and drowned her baby
boy."

I was looking towards the woman at this
moment, and could not refrain from a slight
start at the sudden manner in which a
deeply-lined, awfully white face was raised
from the bent arms, and then as suddenly
buried again, when it met my own turned
in her direction. In that face and in that
brief movement was concentrated her whole
story—and I fancied, in the horror and fear

delineated thereon, I could read the secret that had brought her to the river bank a little while ago.

" And the woman has not been heard of since?"

" No, sir.   There was a matter of fifty pounds offered for her apprehension, but she has never been heard of, sir—the better for all parties, perhaps. The old man gave up after that new trouble, sir; when he lost faith in his darter, he lost faith in everything under the sun. He gave up going to church, to talking with the villagers, and took to loving money instead of his child, like an old miser as he's kept for nigh on twenty years, growing worse with every day. Well," he added, philosophically, as he knocked the ashes out of his pipe against the top bar of the grate; " such a trial as that might turn you or me as much, sir— who can tell?"

" The old man lives entirely alone at the ferry-house?"

" Yes, sir—and people do say he's scraped together a tidy lot of money, by dint of starving, and begging, and ferrying; and that, when he dies, it'll be found hidden about the house in heaps."

"Is he not afraid of thieves?"

"Thieves in Nantle, sir!—I never heard of such a thing."

So this was the story that the old man had declined to tell—I knew now why he did not care to relate the same himself. And it told its moral too—the old moral to the old, old story—that one false step from right may be leaping into a gulf from the depths of which there is no rescue. I could not sleep after its narration—I was painfully wide awake, and the least noise jarred upon my nerves, and made me restless. The woman at the table was a basilisk, from which I could not distract my gaze. I felt that she had been an eager listener, and that she alone of all the world might possibly be able to add further details.

This fancy took so strong a hold upon me that I began to grow anxious for a sight of her white face again—for a chance of studying it in search of that lost beauty that had been her utter ruin. Was it speculative romance or a strange coincidence? Had I indeed been a witness at the ferry to the silent meeting between those whom crime had parted twenty years ago? Twenty years!—and the woman had grey hair now, and the face of a hag—crime had changed her more than time, if she were Jenny Wisford.

I remember that night setting in wet, the heavy drops pelting against the window-glass, and the wind suddenly rising and whirling wildly round the house. I remember listening to the rain, and the sighing of the wind, till the American clock struck two, then three, and the fire burned hollow and collapsed, and the landlord fell asleep with his pipe in his mouth, and his arms folded, bravo fashion, on his chest.

Suddenly I was roused to my feet, and the pipe frightened from the landlord's lip into the fender, by an exclamation from the woman who had so long retained her sleeping posture.

" I can't stop here! I shall go mad if I stop here !"

She had raised her head from the table, on which she had smitten her large hand passionately.

" Hullo here !—what's all this noise about ?" exclaimed the landlord.

" Unlock your door, and let me be going on my way. I have many miles to travel before sunrise."

" Don't you hear the rain, lass ?" said the landlord.

" I'm a tramp, and rough weather does not frighten me. I've roughed it many years now, and I'm not afraid of catching cold and dying of it. No such luck for one sick of life as I am."

"But you have had no rest," I suggested ; "there is a small room upstairs, and I am sure our landlord will allow me to de-fray——"

"I want no man's charity," said the wo-man, rudely, as she snatched her bonnet from the floor. "Unbar the door, and let me out into the night. Don't you hear I must be gone ?"

"Oh ! I don't wish to keep you against your will," said the landlord, becoming warm in his turn ; "only, as you've had shelter here for hours, called for nothing, and been asked for nothing, I would ha' tried and kept a civil tongue. This way, marm."

"You mustn't mind me," said the wo-man, in a milder tone ; " I've seen trouble, and am hasty-like. Thank you for your kindness, though I wish to pay for it."

She began fumbling in the pocket of her tattered gown as she rose to her feet ; but the landlord told her to keep her money—

he wanted none of it, and he had no charge to make for house-room.

"Are you going far?" I ventured to inquire.

"Back to London. I've walked from London every step, on the faith of a fool's dream—but then I'm a mad fool, and a whim leads me anywhere. But oh! that dream!" with a shiver; "it was like a call to be prepared—a warning that there was one chance left me even yet. But I'm mad —stark mad!"

"To start forth in the rain like this— right you be," observed the landlord.

The woman made no answer, but followed the landlord to the door, which was unbarred and open for her egress. Without bidding either of us good night, she stepped across the threshold, drew her shawl round her, and stood for a moment as if doubtful of her way. The landlord had not closed the door, and I was looking over his shoulder at the strange woman who had ventured forth in such rough weather, when the clear, sharp report of a pistol rang suddenly through the air. As the landlord caught me by the arm, and gave vent to an exclamation of surprise, the woman flung up her arms, and came, with a wild scream, back upon us.

"The dream!—the dream! Oh! my God, it's true at last, and he is murdered! I saw it all a week ago—his white hair dabbled with blood, and he lying on his face on the wet grass outside. Oh! is there no one here to help me?" she cried, wringing her hands.

I was about to assert that at present there was little reason for her excitement, when there was wailed faintly from the distance a word that blanched all cheeks, and paralyzed us for a moment with its awful meaning—" *Murder!*"

An instant, and then the woman was running down the lane bare-headed, her bonnet in the roadway; and the landlord had seized a stick and hat from the passage, exclaiming—"There's mischief abroad to-night. Will you follow, sir?"

I ran into the room for my hat, and then the landlord of the "Lion" and I were hastening down the lane after the woman, who sped swiftly on before us, and whom there was no overtaking. As we hurried towards the ferry, voices of people awakened in the village sounded in the rear; and a dog, breaking from its sleep in the coach-yard, came bounding by our side. I have said the distance was not far to the ferry-house; the bend of the lane brought it once more to view—a dark blot near the water's edge, scarcely distinguishable from the darkness of the night. As we neared it, a piercing scream from the woman once more echoed in our ears; and, reaching the place at last, we could distinguish her bending over a prostrate form, *lying on its face on the grass before the ferry-house.*

"Murdered!" gasped the landlord. "This

is a strange and awful night, to be remembered by us both."

" Ay !"

" A light !—a light !—don't stand prating there !" cried the woman. " He is not dead !—I thank my God he is not dead !"

The landlord ran into the ferry-house, and I stooped over the wounded man, and felt for some signs of life about his heart. Something in my manner appeared to suggest my profession to the woman.

" You are a doctor?" she asked, eagerly.

" Yes."

" Will he live, sir ? Do you think there is hope for him even now?"

" It is impossible to say at present."

The landlord had a flint and steel, and was busy, inside the hut, striving hard to obtain a spark from them, when one villager, then another, arrived in breathless haste. When the ferryman's lantern was casting a sickly gleam on the wounded father, and the daughter bending over him, the number of those awakened from their first sleep had increased to eight, three of them shivering, anxious, inquisitive, sympathetic women, ready to offer assistance, or get wet through, or speculate upon the motives of the crime, as circumstances might occur.

Jacob Wisford was laid upon his bed, in the ferry-house, at last; an old lamp, half filled with oil, was discovered on the mantel-piece, and lighted; the men and women came into the room, increased as if by magic, filled the little hut, glared over each other's shoulders in the doorway. The robbers had been busy, and old Jacob Wisford had evidently fought hard before receiving his death-blow. The table and chairs were overturned, a sideboard in one corner had been cleared of its freight of glass and crockery, and the fragments strewn about the floor; the contents of an old chest of drawers had been emptied, and every hole and corner had evidently been ransacked in the search for the little hoard accumulated by many years of miserly thrift, but still of honest labour.

One glance at the old man's face, by the light of the oil-lamp held above it, told of the vanity of human hopes, and of the fleeting nature of human life. A few more minutes, and the world would close with the ferryman, and all be over. There was no need to break the news to her crouching at the bedside, and clutching at the old man's hand, as if her grasp could stay his fleeting soul; a child might have read the story imprinted on that face.

" He will die?" she murmured, looking up at me.

I nodded my head.

" And never know that I am here at last. Oh! my God, if he would only speak once more."

" *The money!*"

It was the answer to her prayer; so quickly and suddenly answered, with the eyes distended, and the disengaged hand grasping so wildly at the air, that more than one stepped back, and changed colour. The woman sprang to her feet, and bent her face close to the murdered man's.

" Father !"

No answer.

" Father, it is Jenny come back. Will you say one word to her ? Will you make some sign ? Your own Jenny !"

" The money ! They have taken it all !"

" Do you know them ?" I asked, quickly.

The old man appeared to understand me, for he shook his head, and sighed. I repeated my question, and he shook his head again.

" Ask him, sir," said the woman, " for mercy's sake ! if he remembers his daughter Jenny—she who broke his heart ?"

At her request, I put the question, and received for answer the old reply,—

" The money !"

Money had been next his heart for twenty years ; in his dying hour, he seemed to love that best on all the earth, and to find it hardest to part with at the last. But the woman made one last heart-rending appeal, and as the word "father" escaped her lips a third time, the dying man's eyes lighted up as with new life, and he made one movement with his hand, as if to push her from him.

" Back !"

" No, no!" shrieked the woman. "Not now, not in the last awful moment we are ever to meet, on earth or in heaven—not now! I have come hundreds of miles to see you once again, to ask your mercy, to tell you I am not so bad; I never was so wholly and unnaturally bad. I didn't kill the child; it fell from my arms, crossing the ferry, and the black water swept it away. It was my bitterest curse to lose it, heaven bear a guilty woman witness! You believe it, you will belie——"

She stopped, and her arms fell heavily, rigidly to her side. Jacob Wisford was dead to all belief for ever. Had he died with the knowledge of his daughter's innocence of that one awful crime with which the world had charged her?—or had he passed from life to death in ignorance? God knows! He had died peacefully, at least, and with a calm smile on his face, that reminded those who had known him, in better times, of the Jacob Wisford of old days, before his daughter stole away from him. Did it matter whether, in that life suddenly ended, he knew all? In the life beyond, do not all the mysteries of our poor humanity vanish away, and all the doubts and cruel mistrusts roll back from the real?

This is my story, ladies and gentlemen. I have little more to say. The assassins of Jacob Wisford were traced, and comfortably hanged. The money—a matter of some hundred and twenty pounds, was harder to discover than the thieves, and passed away no one knows whither—no one ever knows where all the money vanishes!—and the daughter, Jenny, broke up suddenly beneath the shock of that strange night, and was buried in Nantle churchyard, with the ferry-man.

THE END.

LONDON : PRINTED BY MACDONALD AND TUGWELL, BLENHEIM HOUSE

MESSRS. HURST AND BLACKETT'S
LIST OF NEW WORKS.

RECOLLECTIONS OF SOCIETY IN FRANCE
AND ENGLAND. By Lady Clementina Davies. 2 vols. 21s.

Among numerous other distinguished persons referred to in this work are :—Louis XVI, Marie Antoinette, Louis XVIII, the Duchesse D'Angouleme, Napoleon I, the Empress Josephine, Queen Hortense, Charles X, Louis Philippe, the Duke and Duchess de Berry, the Count de Chambord, the Emperor Alexander, King Frederic William, Prince Talleyrand, Prince Esterhazy, Blucher, Ney, Soult, Fouché, the Polignacs, Talma, Napoleon III, the Empress Eugenie, the Duc de Morny, Count d'Orsay, Victor Hugo, George IV, Queen Caroline, Prince Leopold, the Princess Charlotte, the Duke of York, the Duke of Wellington, Lord Byron, Sir Walter Scott, Sir H. Davy, Tom Moore, Mr. Barham, Mrs. Siddons, the Kembles, Mrs. Jordan, Miss Stephens, Mlle. Mars, Madame Catalani, Mlle. Rachel, the Countess Guiccioli, Lady Cork, Lady Blessington, &c.

"To every class of readers, Lady Clementina Davies's work will prove deeply interesting. As a book of anecdotes the volumes will be perused with avidity. Throughout the 'Recollections' we trace the hand of an artist, one whose power and talents are of the highest order, and who has the faculty of bringing before the reader the most striking incidents of the present century in France and England, thus combining the functions of the historian and the biographer with those of the delineator of life as it exists. The style throughout is terse and lively; it abounds with graphic descriptions, and there is an earnestness and a pathos when the authoress flies from gay to grave subjects that touches the heart. Witness the account of Josephine's sanctuary at Malmaison, and the dying hours of the ill-fated Duc de Berri. The lovers of history will be amply repaid by poring over the last days of Marie Antoinette at Versailles; the restoration of Louis XVIII. to the throne of his ancestors; the escape of Napoleon from Elba; and the *Coup d'Etat*. The man about town will revel in those scenes in which Count D'Orsay, Byron, the poet Moore, Lord Petersham, and Sir Charles Wetherall took prominent parts. The patrons of the drama will have Catalani, Mrs. Jordan, John Kemble, the stately Siddons, Talma, Mdlle. Georges, Mdlle. Mars. Mdlle. Duchesnois, Miss Stephens, again brought upon the scene; the gossips will take in with avidity the small-talk of London society, the elopement at Paris; the eccentricities of Lady Cork; in addition to the above we have anecdotes of Walter Scott, Lord Fife, the Prince Regent, the Emperor of Russia, King of Prussia, Louis Philippe, Duchesse d'Orleans, the Bourbons, Talleyrand, Napoleon I. and III., Soult, Wellington, Esterhazy, and M. Thiers. No book of reminiscences, with perhaps one or two exceptions, has left upon us so pleasing an impression as the work under our notice, and which at once stamps Lady Clementina as a most agreeable and clever authoress."—*Court Journal*.

"A book worth reading."—*Examiner*.

"This truly amusing book is thoroughly rich in relation to well-known and highly important persons that played no unimportant part upon the stage of life during the end of the past and also during the present century. The work is as genial as it is comprehensive, and as full of information as it is of wit."—*Messenger*.

"Lady Clementina Davies's Recollections is a book likely to attract much attention. She writes in a pleasant, easy style."—*Scotsman*.

"A singularly interesting and amusing work, full of anecdote, gossip, and life, and giving a whole series of pictures of Paris and London, in a sufficiently exciting epoch. The entire record is full of entertainment."—*Sunday Times*.

"Living as she has done for considerably more than half a century in the very highest circles both here and on the Continent, Lady Clementina Davies has a very wide field to draw on for her social 'Recollections.' There is much in her book that is worth reading, as interesting, or curious, or amusing in some way or another."—*Observer*.

MESSRS. HURST AND BLACKETT'S
NEW WORKS—*Continued.*

THE SWITZERS. By W. Hepworth Dixon.
Author of "New America," "Free Russia," "Her Majestys'
Tower," &c. *Third Edition.* 1 vol. demy 8vo. 15s.

Contents:—Mountain Men; St. Gothard; Peopling the Alps; The Fight for Life;
Rain and Rocks; Teuton and Celt; The Communes; Communal Authorities;
Communal Government; Cantons and Half Cantons; Cantonal Rule; Canton
Zürich; Pure Democracy; A Revolution; Popular Victories; The League;
The Federal Pact; Jesuits; Pilgrimage; Convent and Canton; St. Meinrad's
Cell; Feast of the Rosary; Last of the Benedictines; Conflict of the Churches;
School; Democracy at School; Geneva; Scheme of Work; Secondary Schools;
School and Camp; Defence; The Public Force; In the Field; Out Again; A
Crowning Service.

"Turn where we will there is the same impassioned eloquence, the same lavish
wealth of metaphor, the same vigour of declamation, the same general glow upon
the pages. Switzerland may be hackneyed as a country, yet there is freshness in
Mr. Dixon's subjects. Mr. Dixon throws a passing glance at the snow peaks and
glacier fields that are the Switzerland of the tourist. If he deals with the grand
catastrophes of nature, with avalanche, flood, and storm, it is in their relation
to the victims of the elements, for his topics are the people and their institutions.
We assent entirely to the parable of his preface."—*Times.*

"A lively, interesting, and altogether novel book on Switzerland. It is full of
valuable information on social, political, and ecclesiastical questions, and, like all
Mr. Dixon's books, it is eminently readable."—*Daily News.*

"We advise every one who cares for good literature to get a copy of this brilliant,
novel, and abundantly instructive account of the Switzers. The composition of the
book is in the very best style."—*Morning Post.*

"A work of real and abiding value. Mr. Dixon has never painted with more
force and truth. His descriptions are accurate, impartial, and clear. We most
cordially recommend the book."—*Standard.*

"A most interesting and useful work; especially well timed when the questions
of military organization and primary education occupy so large a share of public
attention. There is that happy fusion of the picturesque and the practical in Mr.
Dixon's works which gives especially to the present book its great charm. It has
at once the graphic interest of a romance, and the sterling value of an educational
essay."—*Daily Telegraph.*

"Mr. Dixon has succeeded in giving the public a very inviting book. The reader
rises from it with the pleasant consciousness of having acquired useful information
without fatigue, and of having been as much interested by solid truth as if it were
fiction meant only to amuse."—*Echo.*

"Any respectable book on the Switzers and Switzerland is welcome to lovers of
the land and the people, and we trust that Mr. Dixon's volume will be read in Switzerland as well as in England."—*Athenæum.*

"Mr. Dixon's book contains much readable and instructive matter."—*Examiner.*

"A writer of much dramatic and descriptive power, and one who knows his way
to trustworthy sources of information, Mr. Dixon has given a clever and instructive
sketch of the salient features of the confederation. All who know the playground
of Europe will thank the writer for so clear an account of the social institutions of
a free people."—*Graphic.*

"This work is in every respect the most useful and the best by means of which
Mr. Dixon has introduced novel subjects all worthy of the utmost attention of his
countrymen, and illustrated them by so elegant a method of communication as immensely to enhance their value."—*Messenger.*

"No such book has been written concerning Switzerland by any Englishman,
and few books of travel we possess unite more valuable information to more descriptive power and charm of style."—*Sunday Times.*

MESSRS. HURST AND BLACKETT'S
NEW WORKS—*Continued.*

MODERN TURKEY. By J. Lewis Farley,
Consul of the Sublime Porte at Bristol. *Second Edition.* 1 vol. 14s.

Contents:—Beyront; Beit-Miry; Mount Lebanon; Travelling in Syria and Palestine; a Day with the Bedawins; Syria, Past and Present; the Empress Eugénie's Visit to Constantinople; the Suez Canal; Turkish Women; Turkish Armaments: Public Instruction; the Capitulations; Turkey as a Field for Emigration; British Interests in Turkey; Turkish Finances: the Stock Exchange; Geographical Position of the Empire; Agricultural Products; Fisheries; Mines; Petroleum; Roads; Railways; Docks and Harbours! Public Works, &c

"'Modern Turkey,' by J. Lewis Farley, is from a writer long familiar with the country, and whose experience encourages a sanguine view of its future, alike as regards social, political, and industrial advancement."—*Times.*

"Mr. Farley has a good deal of interesting information to communicate in regard to the resources of modern Turkey; and we may add that he puts it briefly, clearly, and in an agreeable style."—*Saturday Review.*

"Mr. Farley is to be praised for the admirable manner in which he has marshalled his facts and arranged his matter. His style, too, is lucid and agreeable, and he manages to clothe the dry skeleton of statistics with life and animation. His book will do a great deal to remove many prejudices against Turkey from the minds of Englishmen, and will bring very vividly before their eyes the present condition of a country about which great numbers of our countrymen are lamentably ignorant."—*Examiner.*

"This very interesting and exceedingly well-written volume well deserves an earnest perusal. It is a book of incalculable value to every class of the community."—*Messenger.*

"An able sketch of the present state and latest resources of the Ottoman Empire. Mr. Farley writes ably and clearly, and few will put down his book without having learned something new about the material resources of Turkey, and the aspirations of its most enlightened statesmen."—*Graphic.*

"It is quite pleasant to fall in with a book of this kind. Mr. Farley was for some time a resident in Turkey, and has a good deal worth hearing to say about the country."—*Globe.*

"Mr. Farley evinces a thorough knowledge of his subject, and his work deserves to be attentively perused by all who are interested politically, commercially, or financially, in the Ottoman Empire."—*Liverpool Albion.*

"A very charming, useful, and readable book, which we can cordially recommend to all who wish to increase their knowledge of the Turkish Empire."—*Birmingham News.*

HISTORY OF WILLIAM PENN, Founder of
Pennsylvania. By W. Hepworth Dixon. A New Library Edition. 1 vol. demy 8vo, with Portrait. 12s.

"Mr. Dixon's 'William Penn' is, perhaps, the best of his books. He has now revised and issued it with the addition of much fresh matter. It is now offered in a sumptuous volume, matching with Mr. Dixon's recent books, to a new generation of readers, who will thank Mr. Dixon for his interesting and instructive memoir of one of the worthies of England."—*Examiner.*

"'William Penn' is a fine and noble work. Eloquent, picturesque, and epigramatic in style, subtle and philosophical in insight, and moderate and accurate in statement, it is a model of what a biography ought to be."—*Sunday Times.*

"The character of this great Christian Englishman, William Penn, a true hero of moral and civil conquests, is one of the fairest in modern history, and may be studied with profit by his countrymen of all ages. This biography of him now finally put into shape as a standard work of its kind, is Mr. Dixon's most useful production. Few books have a more genial and wholesome interest, or convey more beneficial instruction."—*Illustrated News.*

"Like all Mr. Dixon's books this is written in a pleasing, popular style, and at the present moment, when our relations with the United States are attracting so much attention to the Great Republic of the new world, the re-appearance is most timely and welcome."—*Echo.*

"One of the most able specimens of biography that has ever appeared."—*Messenger.*

MESSRS. HURST AND BLACKETT'S
NEW WORKS—*Continued.*

SPORT AT HOME AND ABROAD. By LORD
WILLIAM PITT LENNOX. 2 vols. crown 8vo. 21s.

"Two very amusing and instructive volumes, touching on all sorts of sport, from the experienced pen of a writer well qualified to handle the subject. Stored with interesting matter the book will take the fancy of all lovers of pastime by flood or field."—*Bell's Life.*

"This work is extremely interesting and instructive from the first page to the last. It contains a vast amount of useful information and excellent advice for the British sportsman. interspersed with an inexhaustible fund of anecdote."—*Court Journal.*

"Lovers of sport will welcome this new work by Lord W. Lennox eagerly. We have here experiences of sport of the most varied kind—from fishing in Upper Canada to fowling in Siberia; from Highland deer hunting to angling on the quiet banks of the Thames. Then descriptions of ancient and modern gymnastics, sports of England in the middle ages, hunting, fencing, wrestling, cricketing, and cock-fighting. We may learn how to choose a yacht or a hound, a hunter or a rifle, from these useful and amusing pages. And there are also a great number of lively anecdotes to amuse the 'noble sportsman' when the fish won't rise, when the deer are shy, or the weather is unfavourable. or there is a dead calm for the yacht. We predict a great success for this book."—*Era.*

PRAIRIE FARMS AND PRAIRIE FOLK. By
PARKER GILLMORE ("Ubique"), Author of "A Hunter's Adventures in the Great West," &c. 2 vols crown 8vo, with Illustrations. 21s.

"Mr. Gillmore has written a book which will make the English reader take a deep interest in Prairie Farms and Prairie Folk. His narrative of his sojourn, his description of the country, and of his neighbours, are all most readable. Mr. Gillmore's sporting feats are the themes of some of its best chapters."—*Daily News.*

"This work is the very best of its class that Mr. Parker Gillmore has yet written, not merely because of its lifelike descriptions of open-air life in the vast outlying districts of the American continent, but because it gives an amount of information of incalculable value to emigrants."—*Messenger.*

"For anecdotes, descriptions, and all kinds of information relating to sport it would not be easy to name a more effective and readable writer than Parker Gillmore."—*Illustrated London News.*

"We heartily recommend this work. The attraction of the author's descriptions is very great. His style is graphic, and his records are always entertaining and remarkable."—*Sunday Times.*

QUEEN CHARLOTTE ISLANDS: A Narrative
of Discovery and Adventure in THE NORTH PACIFIC. By FRANCIS POOLE, C.E. Edited by JOHN W. LYNDON. 1 vol. 8vo, with Map and Illustrations. 15s.

"There can be no doubt whatever about the spirit of enterprise and power of endurance with which Mr. Poole is gifted, and much of his book is very exciting reading. Nor are the parts of it which are the least novel the least interesting; and the chapters descriptive of his journeys to and fro, round America, and across the Isthmus, with his account of San Francisco and Victoria, will repay perusal. The materials Mr. Poole furnished have been edited by Mr. John W. Lyndon. Mr. Lyndon seems to have discharged his office with commendable judgment."—*Pall Mall Gazette.*

"As a whole the book is interesting and instructive, and its author evidently a pleasant and a plucky fellow. We can confidently recommend the book to all who wish to form an idea of life and land in those countries in the present, and of their capacity in the future."—*Athenæum.*

"This very interesting narrative is excellent reading. Mr. Poole has added much that is valuable to the stock of general information."—*Daily News.*

"This extremely interesting work—well written and well edited—is full of novelty and curious facts. It is one among the most fresh and instructive volumes of travel and adventure which have been produced for a long time."—*Standard.*

MESSRS. HURST AND BLACKETT'S
NEW WORKS—*Continued.*

THE LITERARY LIFE OF THE REV. WILLIAM HARNESS, Vicar of All Saints, Knightsbridge, and Prebendary of St. Paul's. By the Rev. A. G. L'Estrange. 8vo. 15s.

Among other celebrated persons of whom anecdotes and reminiscences will be found in this work are Lord Byron, Sheridan, Scott, Crabbe. Coleridge, Moore, Rogers, Charles Lamb, Sydney Smith, Talfourd, Theodore Hook, Dickens, Thackeray, Lockhart, Lady Byron, Miss Mitford, Miss Austen, Joanna Baillie, Mrs Siddons, Madame d'Arblay, &c.

"The book is a pleasant book, and will be found excellent reading. All those to whom the good name of Byron is dear, to the utmost extent of its desert, will read with an almost exquisite pleasure the testimony given by Harness. The fine qualities of the man are set forth, without any attempt to conceal his errors or his vices; as regards the latter, there is shown to have been gross exaggeration in the report of them."—*Athenæum.*

" We are sure that this work will be read with much interest. The Rev. William Harness was the friend of Byron, and of almost every literary celebrity of his time. He liked to be about literary men, and they reciprocated that liking. Byron. Miss Mitford, the Kembles, Wordsworth, Southey, Coleridge, Lamb, Rogers, Sheridan, Theodore Hook, Henry Hope, were among his friends; and the consequence of this varied literary friendship is that his life, for richness in biographical details, is surpassed by no recent publication except Crabb Robinson's Diary."— *The Echo.*

LIFE AND LETTERS OF WILLIAM BEWICK, THE ARTIST. Edited by Thomas Landseer, A.R.A. 2 vols. large post 8vo, with Portrait. 24s.

"Mr. Landseer seems to have had a pious pleasure in editing this biography and these letters of his old friend We should be wanting in our duty were we not to thank him for furnishing us with such interesting memorials of a man who did good work in his generation, but about whom so little is known."—*Times.*

"Mr. Landseer's account of Bewick's life is altogether interesting. The volumes are a pleasant medley of autobiographical fragments, letters, literary criticisms, and anecdotes, judiciously strung together by Mr. Landseer with concise links of narrative, and the whole work gives a lively and most welcome view of the character and career of a man who is worth remembering on his own account, and yet more on account of the friends and great men with whom he associated. There are very welcome references to Haydon, Wilkie, Wordsworth, Ugo Foscolo, Hazlitt, Sir Walter Scott, the Ettrick Shepherd, Shelley, Keats, Leigh Hunt, and a score or more of other men of whom the world can hardly hear too much."—*Examiner.*

"The interest for general readers of this 'Life and Letters ' is derived almost entirely from anecdotes of men of mark with whom the artist associated, and of which it contains a very large and amusing store. His fellow pupil and old friend, Mr. Thomas Landseer, the famous engraver. has put the materials before us together with much skill and a great deal of genial tact. The literary sketches which Bewick made of Hazlitt, Haydon, Shelley, Keats, Scott, Hogg, Jeffrey, Maturin, and others, are extremely bright, apt, and clear."—*Athenæum.*

TURKISH HAREMS & CIRCASSIAN HOMES.
By Mrs. Harvey, of Ickwell Bury. 8vo. *Second Edition.* 15s.

"Mrs. Harvey's book could scarcely fail to be pleasant, for the excursion of which it gives us an account must have been one of the most delightful and romantic voyages that ever was made. Mrs. Harvey not only saw a great deal, but saw all that she did see to the best advantage. She was admitted into Turkish interiors which are rarely penetrated, and, protected by an escort, was able to ride far into the mountains of Circassia, whose lovely defiles are full of dangers which seal them to ordinary travellers. We cannot call to mind any account written of late years which is so full of valuable information upon Turkish household life. In noticing the intrinsic interest of Mrs. Harvey's book, we must not forget to say a word for her ability as a writer."—*Times.*

MESSRS. HURST AND BLACKETT'S
NEW WORKS—*Continued.*

VOLS. I. & II. OF HER MAJESTY'S TOWER.
By W. HEPWORTH DIXON. DEDICATED BY EXPRESS PERMISSION TO THE QUEEN. *Sixth Edition.* 8vo. 30s.

CONTENTS:—The Pile—Inner Ward and Outer Ward—The Wharf—River Rights—The White Tower—Charles of Orleans—Uncle Gloucester—Prison Rules—Beauchamp Tower—The good Lord Cobham—King and Cardinal—The Pilgrimage of Grace—Madge Cheyne—Heirs to the Crown—The Nine Days' Queen—Dethroned—The Men of Kent—Courtney—No Cross no Crown—Cranmer, Latimer, Ridley—White Roses—Princess Margaret—Plot and Counterplot—Monsieur Charles—Bishop of Ross—Murder of Northumberland—Philip the Confessor—Mass in the Tower—Sir Walter Raleigh—The Arabella Plot—Raleigh's Walk—The Villain Waad—The Garden House—The Brick Tower—The Anglo-Spanish Plot—Factions at Court—Lord Grey of Wilton—Old English Catholics—The English Jesuits—White Webbs—The Priests' Plot—Wilton Court—Last of a Noble Line—Powder-Plot Room—Guy Fawkes—Origin of the Plot—Vinegar House—Conspiracy at Large—The Jesuit's Move—In London—November, 1605—Hunted Down—In the Tower—Search for Garnet—End of the English Jesuits—The Catholic Lords—Harry Percy—The Wizard Earl—A Real Arabella Plot—William Seymour—The Escape—Pursuit—Dead in the Tower—Lady Frances Howard—Robert Carr—Powder Poisoning.

FROM THE TIMES:—"All the civilized world—English, Continental, and American—takes an interest in the Tower of London. The Tower is the stage upon which has been enacted some of the grandest dramas and saddest tragedies in our national annals. If, in imagination, we take our stand on those time-worn walls, and let century after century flit past us, we shall see in due succession the majority of the most famous men and lovely women of England in the olden time. We shall see them jesting, jousting, love-making, plotting, and then anon, perhaps, commending their souls to God in the presence of a hideous masked figure, bearing an axe in his hands. It is such pictures as these that Mr. Dixon, with considerable skill as an historical limner, has set before us in these volumes. Mr. Dixon dashes off the scenes of Tower history with great spirit. His descriptions are given with such terseness and vigour that we should spoil them by any attempt at condensation. As favourable examples of his narrative powers we may call attention to the story of the beautiful but unpopular Elinor, Queen of Henry III., and the description of Anne Boleyn's first and second arrivals at the Tower. Then we have the story of the bold Bishop of Durham, who escapes by the aid of a cord hidden in a wine-jar; and the tale of Maud Fitzwalter, imprisoned and murdered by the caitiff John. Passing onwards, we meet Charles of Orleans, the poetic French Prince, captured at Agincourt, and detained for five-and-twenty years a prisoner in the Tower. Next we encounter the baleful form of Richard of Gloucester, and are filled with indignation at the blackest of the black Tower deeds. As we draw nearer to modern times, we have the sorrowful story of the Nine Days' Queen, poor little Lady Jane Grey. The chapter entitled "No Cross, no Crown" is one of the most affecting in the book. A mature man can scarcely read it without feeling the tears ready to trickle from his eyes. No part of the first volume yields in interest to the chapters which are devoted to the story of Sir Walter Raleigh. The greater part of the second volume is occupied with the story of the Gunpowder Plot. The narrative is extremely interesting, and will repay perusal. Another *cause célébre* possessed of a perennial interest, is the murder of Sir Thomas Overbury by Lord and Lady Somerset. Mr. Dixon tells the tale skilfully. In conclusion, we may congratulate the author on this work. Both volumes are decidedly attractive, and throw much light on our national history."

"From first to last this work overflows with new information and original thought, with poetry and picture. In these fascinating pages Mr. Dixon discharges alternately the functions of the historian, and the historic biographer, with the insight, art, humour and accurate knowledge which never fail him when he undertakes to illumine the darksome recesses of our national story."—*Morning Post.*

"We earnestly recommend this remarkable work to those in quest of amusement and instruction, at once solid and refined.."—*Daily Telegraph.*

MESSRS. HURST AND BLACKETT'S
NEW WORKS—*Continued.*

VOLS. III. & IV. OF HER MAJESTY'S TOWER.
By W. HEPWORTH DIXON.   DEDICATED BY EXPRESS
PERMISSION TO THE QUEEN.   Completing the Work.   *Third
Edition.*   Demy 8vo.   30s.

CONTENTS:—A Favourite; A Favourite's Friend; The Countess of Suffolk; To the
Tower; Lady Catherine Manners; House of Villiers; Revolution; Fall of Lord
Bacon; A Spanish Match; Spaniolizing; Henry De Vere; The Matter of Hol-
land; Sea Affairs; The Pirate War; Port and Court; A New Romanzo; Move
and Counter-move; Pirate and Prison; In the Marshalsea; The Spanish Olive;
Prisons Opened; A Parliament; Digby, Earl of Bristol; Turn of Fortune; Eliot
Eloquent; Felton's Knife; An Assassin; Nine Gentlemen in the Tower; A
King's Revenge; Charles I.; Pillars of State and Church; End of Wentworth;
Laud's Last Troubles; The Lieutenant's House; A Political Romance; Phi-
losophy at Bay; Fate of an Idealist; Britannia; Killing not Murder; A Second
Buckingham; Roger, Earl of Castlemaine; A Life of Plots; The Two Penns;
A Quaker's Cell; Colonel Blood; Crown Jewels, King and Colonel; Rye House
Plot; Murder; A Patriot; The Good Old Cause; James, Duke of Monmouth;
The Unjust Judge; The Scottish Lords; The Countess of Nithisdale; Escaped;
Cause of the Pretender; Reformers and Reform, Reform Riots; Sir Francis
Burdett; A Summons to the Tower; Arthur Thistlewood; A Cabinet Council;
Cato Street; Pursuit; Last Prisoners in the Tower.

" Mr. Dixon's lively and accurate work."—*Times.*

" This book is thoroughly entertaining, well-written, and instructive."—*Examiner.*

" These volumes will place Mr. Dixon permanently on the roll of English authors
who have rendered their country a service, by his putting on record a truthful and
brilliant account of that most popular and instructive relic of antiquity. ' Her
Majesty's Tower;' the annals of which, as related in these volumes, are by turns
exciting and amusing, while they never fail to interest. Our ancient stronghold
could have had no better historian than Mr. Dixon."—*Post.*

" By his merits of literary execution, his vivacious portraitures of historical
figures, his masterly powers of narrative and description, and the force and graceful ease of his style, Mr. Dixon will keep his hold upon a multitude of readers."—
Illustrated News.

" These volumes are two galleries of richly painted portraits of the noblest
men and most brilliant women, besides others commemorated by English
history. The grand old Royal Keep, palace and prison by turns, is revivified in
these volumes, which close the narrative, extending from the era of Sir John Eliot,
who saw Raleigh die in Palace Yard, to that of Thistlewood, the last prisoner im-
mured in the Tower. Few works are given to us, in these days, so abundant in
originality and research as Mr. Dixon's."—*Standard.*

" This intensely interesting work will become as popular as any book Mr.
Dixon has written."—*Messenger.*

" A work always eminently readable, often of fascinating interest."—*Echo.*

" The most brilliant and fascinating of Mr. Dixon's literary achievements."—*Sun.*

" Mr. Dixon has accomplished his task well. Few subjects of higher and more
general interest than the Tower could have been found. Around the old pile
clings all that is most romantic in our history. To have made himself the trusted
and accepted historian of the Tower is a task on which a writer of highest reputation may well be proud. This Mr. Dixon has done. He has, moreover, adapted
his work to all classes. To the historical student it presents the result of long
and successful research in sources undiscovered till now; to the artist it gives the
most glowing picture yet, perhaps, produced of the more exciting scenes of national
history; to the general reader it offers fact with all the graces of fiction. Mr.
Dixon's book is admirable alike for the general view of history it presents, and for
the beauty and value of its single pictures."—*Sunday Times.*

MESSRS HURST AND BLACKETT'S
NEW WORKS—*Continued.*

FREE RUSSIA. By W. HEPWORTH DIXON. *Third Edition* 2 vols. 8vo, with Coloured Illustrations. 30s.

"Mr. Dixon's book will be certain not only to interest but to please its readers and it deserves to do so. It contains a great deal that is worthy of attention, and is likely to produce a very useful effect. The ignorance of the English people with respect to Russia has long been so dense that we cannot avoid being grateful to a writer who has taken the trouble to make personal acquaintance with that seldom-visited land, and to bring before the eyes of his countrymen a picture of its scenery and its people, which is so novel and interesting that it can scarcely fail to arrest their attention."—*Saturday Review.*

"Mr. Dixon has invented a good title for his volumes on Russia. The chapter on Lomonosoff, the peasant poet, is one of the best in the book, and the chapter on Kief is equally good. The descriptions of the peasant villages, and of the habits and manners of the peasantry, are very good; in fact, the descriptions are excellent throughout the work."—*Times.*

"We claim for Mr. Dixon the merit of having treated his subject in a fresh and original manner. He has done his best to see with his own eyes the vast country which he describes, and he has visited some parts of the land with which few even among its natives are familiar, and he has had the advantage of being brought into personal contact with a number of those Russians whose opinions are of most weight. The consequence is, that he has been able to lay before general readers such a picture of Russia and the Russian people as cannot fail to interest them."—*Athenæum.*

ANNALS OF OXFORD. By J. C. JEAFFRESON, B.A., Oxon. Author of "A Book About the Clergy," &c. *Second Edition.* 2 vols. 8vo. 30s.

CONTENTS:—The Cross Keys; King Alfred's Expulsion from Oxford; Chums and Inmates; Classical Schools and Benefactions; Schools and Scholars; On Learning and certain Incentives to it; Colleges and Halls; Structural Newness of Oxford; Arithmetic gone Mad; Reduction of the Estimates; A Happy Family; Town and Gown; Death to the Legate's Cook; The Great Riot; St. Scholastica; King's College Chapel used as a Playhouse; St. Mary's Church; Ladies in Residence; Gownswomen of the 17th Century; The Birch in the Bodleian; Aularian Rigour; Royal Smiles: Tudor, Georgian, Elizabeth and Stuart; Royal Pomps; Oxford in Arms; The Cavaliers in Oxford; Henrietta Maria's Triumph and Oxford's Capitulation; The Saints Triumphant; Cromwellian Oxford; Alma Mater in the Days of the Merry Monarch; The Sheldonian Theatre; Gardens and Walks; Oxford Jokes and Sausages; Terræ Filii; The Constitution Club; Nicholas Amhurst; Commemoration; Oxford in the Future.

"The pleasantest and most informing book about Oxford that has ever been written. Whilst these volumes will be eagerly perused by the sons of Alma Mater, they will be read with scarcely less interest by the general reader."—*Post.*

"Those who turn to Mr. Jeaffreson's highly interesting work for solid information or for amusement, will not be disappointed. Rich in research and full of antiquarian interest, these volumes abound in keen humour and well-bred wit. A scholar-like fancy brightens every page. Mr. Jeaffreson is a very model of a cicerone; full of information, full of knowledge. The work well deserves to be read, and merits a permanent niche in the library."—*The Graphic.*

"These interesting volumes should be read not only by Oxonians, but by all students of English history."—*John Bull.*

A BOOK ABOUT THE CLERGY. By J. C. JEAFFRESON, B.A., Oxon, author of "A Book about Lawyers," "A Book about Doctors," &c. *Second Edition.* 2 vols 8vo. 30s.

"This is a book of sterling excellence, in which all—laity as well as clergy—will find entertainment and instruction: a book to be bought and placed permanently in our libraries. It is written in a terse and lively style throughout, it is eminently fair and candid, and is full of interesting information on almost every topic that serves to illustrate the history of the English clergy"—*Times.*

MESSRS. HURST AND BLACKETT'S
NEW WORKS—*Continued.*

MY EXPERIENCES OF THE WAR BETWEEN
FRANCE AND GERMANY. By Archibald Forbes. 2 vols. 8vo.

"Mr. Forbes's book is an extremely valuable contribution to the literature of the War. Not only is the book good in itself but it describes events which have no parallel in modern history."—*Athenæum.*

SPIRITUAL WIVES. By W. Hepworth Dixon.
Fourth Edition. 2 vols. 8vo. With Portrait of the Author. 30s.

"Mr. Dixon has treated his subject in a philosophical spirit, and in his usual graphic manner. There is, to our thinking, more pernicious doctrine in one chapter of some of the sensational novels which find admirers in drawing-rooms and eulogists in the press than in the whole of Mr. Dixon's interesting work."—*Examiner.*

THE CITIES OF THE NATIONS FELL. By
the Rev. John Cumming, D.D. *Second Edition.* 1 vol. 6s.

Contents:—Babylon—Egypt—Nineveh—Tyre and Sidon—Bashan—Jerusalem—Rome—The Seven Cities of Asia—Constantinople—Metz, Sedan, and Strasburg—Vienna—Munich—Madrid—Paris—Chicago—The City that never Falls—The City that comes down from Heaven—There shall be no more Tears—Elements of National Prosperity.

"Dr. Cumming's book will be read by many with advantage."—*Graphic.*

"The work before us contains much historical information of interest and value. We must applaud here, as we applauded in his treatise on The Seventh Vial, the skill and diligence of the author in the vast and careful selection of facts, both physical and moral, the interest of each when taken singly, and the striking picture of the whole when presented collectively to the view."—*Record.*

TRAVELS OF A NATURALIST IN JAPAN
AND MANCHURIA. By Arthur Adams, F.L.S., Staff-Surgeon R.N. 1 vol. 8vo, with Illustrations.

"An amusing volume. Mr Adams has acquired a body of interesting information, which he has set forth in a lively and agreeable style. The book will be a favourite with naturalists, and is calculated to interest others as well."—*Daily News.*

THE SEVENTH VIAL; OR, THE TIME OF
TROUBLE BEGUN, as shown in THE GREAT WAR, THE DETHRONEMENT OF THE POPE, and other Collateral Events. By the Rev. John Cumming, D.D., &c. *Third Edition.* 1 vol. 6s.

"Dr. Cumming is the popular exponent of a school of prophetic interpretation, and on this score has established a claim to attention. His book furnishes an instructive collection of the many strange portents of our day. Dr. Cumming takes his facts very fairly. He has a case, and the gravity of the subject must command the attention of readers."—*Times.*

MEMOIRS OF QUEEN HORTENSE, MOTHER
OF NAPOLEON III. Cheaper Edition, in 1 vol. 6s.

"A biography of the beautiful and unhappy Queen, more satisfactory than any we have yet met with."—*Daily News.*

THE LADYE SHAKERLEY; being the Record of
the Life of a Good and Noble Woman. A Cheshire Story. By ONE of the HOUSE of EGERTON. *Second Edition.* 1 vol. 6s.

"This charming novelette pleasantly reminds one of the well-known series of stories by the author of 'Mary Powell.' The characters bear the same impress of truthfulness, and the reader is made to feel equally at home among scenes sketched with a ready hand. The author writes gracefully, and has the faculty of placing before others the pictures her own imagination has called up."—*Pall Mall Gazette.*

THE NEW AND POPULAR NOVELS
PUBLISHED BY HURST & BLACKETT.

WRAYFORD'S WARD, and other Tales. By F. W. ROBINSON, author of "Grandmother's Money," &c. 3 vols.

THE WOMAN WITH A SECRET. By ALICE KING, author of "Queen of Herself," &c. 3 vols.

JANET'S CHOICE. By MARY CHARLOTTE PHILL-POTTS, author of "Maggie's Secret," &c. 3 vols.

"A delightful story, belonging to that pattern of which Miss Austen was the most finished illustrator."—*Messenger.*

OFF PARADE. By STEPHEN J. MAC KENNA, late 28th Regiment. 3 vols.

"This book teems with interest from the first page to the last. We cannot too strongly recommend 'Off Parade' to all readers, and more especially to young officers in the army, who, in its pages, will find much to interest and even more to edify and instruct. It is a novel which we feel confident will be read alike with pleasure and profit either in camp or in quarters, and we congratulate the author on such a meritorious production, a production equally honourable to his head and heart."—*United Service Magazine.*

"There is nowhere a wider or a brighter field for the social novelist than the British officer's mess-room. Mr. Mac Kenna's officers are life-like, and talk exactly as their compeers may be heard to do any day at Aldershot, or Colchester, or the Curragh. Their rattle is agreeable, and their love-making fairly interesting. There is not a heavy chapter in the book."—*United Service Gazette.*

FIRST IN THE FIELD. By the Author of "Recommended to Mercy." 3 vols.

"A novel of considerable ability..... The plot is full of strong situations. The characters are distinct, and not unnatural."—*Athenæum.*——"We cordially recommend this work for general perusal. The characters are strongly drawn, the incidents well developed and diversified."—*Messenger.*——"A powerful, original, and profoundly interesting novel."—*Sunday Times.*

THE LOST BRIDE. By GEORGIANA LADY CHATTERTON. 3 vols.

"This book is pleasant reading, and ought to satisfy many tastes."—*Examiner.*—"An ingenious and pituresque story, in which there is a good deal of character drawing, and some pleasant and lively sketches of society occur."—*Spectator.*——"'The Lost Bride' will add considerably to Lady Chatterton's literary reputation. It is replete with interest, and the characters are perfectly true to nature."—*Court Journal.*——"Those who read this novel with a facility to sympathize with romance, will, no doubt, be gratified, and all will allow that its purpose and moral are good."--*Post.*

GOLDEN KEYS. 3 vols.

"'Golden Keys' will find a wide circle of readers. It possesses many decided merits, many signs of careful thought and study of character, and a bold healthiness of style and tone. The plot is well planned, and the interest admirably sustained to the last. The various dramatis personæ are drawn with a keen and life-like vigour."—*Standard.*

"The work of a very clever writer and an original thinker."—*John Bull.*

LIL. By JEAN MIDDLEMASS. 3 vols.

"A very readable novel. There is much that is interesting in the history of 'Lil'"—*Examiner.*——"This story is well told. The interest never flags, but fascinates the reader from the very first page to the last."—*Court Journal.*——"'Lil' has many of the qualities of a good novel. The story has the merit of being animated, and well calculated to keep the interest of the reader alive."—*Graphic.*

THE NEW AND POPULAR NOVELS
PUBLISHED BY HURST & BLACKETT.

OMBRA. By Mrs. OLIPHANT. Author of "Chronicles of Carlingford," "Salem Chapel," &c. 3 vols.

"A delightful book."—*Morning Post.*

A GOLDEN SORROW. By Mrs. CASHEL HOEY. 3 v.

"A most agreeable book. Mrs. Hoey not only displays good nature and good sense, but her diction is fresh, clear, and incisive. She weaves an interesting plot, and her characters are drawn with remarkable distinctness and consistency."—*Examiner.*——"A story of remarkable ability both in design and execution, and we much mistake if it does not become one of the most popular novels of the season."—*Graphic.*——"A most admirable novel."—*John Bull.*——"A very pleasant, lively novel."—*Spectator.*

HOPE DEFERRED. By ELIZA F. POLLARD. 3 v.

"We direct attention to this book as a true and beautiful delineation of a woman's heart at war with circumstances and fate. The style is clear and pleasant, and it has an unaffected earnestness—one of the rarest graces of fiction."—*Spectator.*

"We have read few stories lately, certainly none professing to treat of female character, which have left upon us so pleasing an impression."—*Athenæum*

THE QUEEN OF THE REGIMENT. By KATHA-RINE KING. 3 vols.

"A charming, fresh, cheery novel. Its merits are rare and welcome. The glee-fulness, the ease, the heartiness of the Author's style cannot fail to please. Her heroine is a captivating girl."—*Spectator.*——"In spite of little defects, 'The Queen of the Regiment' may be pronounced a successful and attractive novel. It is amusing, and, to some extent, original; the style is simple and unaffected, and the tone is healthy throughout."—*Athenæum.*——"A brilliant novel. The heroine is a charming creature. With the exception of 'Fair to See,' we have not seen any modern novel which shows such intimate acquaintance with, as well as keen observation of, English military life as the book before us."—*United Service Gazette.*

ASTON-ROYAL. By the Author of "St. Olave's." 3 v.

"A book that is delightful to read."—*Post.*——"'Aston-Royal' abounds with beauties, much clever writing, and that thorough insight into human nature which made 'St. Olave's' so universally and deservedly popular."—*Messenger.*

"'Aston Royal' is far superior to anything the author has yet done. The book is not only interesting as a story, but evinces great knowledge of the world and shrewdness of observation."—*British Quarterly Review.*

BRUNA'S REVENGE. By the Author of "Caste," &c. 3 vols.

"Viewed simply as love stories, fresh, pure, and pathetic, these volumes deserve praise."—*Athenæum.*——"'Bruna's Revenge' is all fire, animation, life and reality. The whole story fascinates the reader's attention."—*Standard.*

A WOMAN IN SPITE OF HERSELF. By J. C. JEAFFRESON, Author of "Live it Down," &c. 3 vols.

"A delightful and exciting story. The interest intensifies with every page, until it becomes quite absorbing."—*Morning Post.*

HANNAH. By the Author of "John Halifax." New and Cheaper Edition, in 1 vol. 5s. bound and Illustrated.

"A very pleasant, healthy story, well and artistically told. The book is sure of a wide circle of readers. The character of Hannah is one of rare beauty."—*Standard.*

MY LITTLE LADY. 3 vols.

"There is a great deal of fascination about this book."—*Times.*

HURST & BLACKETT'S STANDARD LIBRARY

OF CHEAP EDITIONS OF

POPULAR MODERN WORKS,

ILLUSTRATED BY MILLAIS, HOLMAN HUNT, LEECH, BIRKET FOSTER,

JOHN GILBERT, TENNIEL, SANDYS, E. HUGHES, &c.

Each in a Single Volume, elegantly printed, bound, and illustrated, price 5s.

I.—SAM SLICK'S NATURE AND HUMAN NATURE.

"The first volume of Messrs. Hurst and Blackett's Standard Library of Cheap Editions forms a very good beginning to what will doubtless be a very successful undertaking. 'Nature and Human Nature' is one of the best of Sam Slick's witty and humorous productions, and is well entitled to the large circulation which it cannot fail to obtain in its present convenient and cheap shape. The volume combines with the great recommendations of a clear, bold type, and good paper, the lesser but attractive merits of being well illustrated and elegantly bound."—*Post.*

II.—JOHN HALIFAX, GENTLEMAN.

"This is a very good and a very interesting work. It is designed to trace the career from boyhood to age of a perfect man—a Christian gentleman; and it abounds in incident both well and highly wrought. Throughout it is conceived in a high spirit, and written with great ability. This cheap and handsome new edition is worthy to pass freely from hand to hand as a gift book in many households."—*Examiner.*

"The new and cheaper edition of this interesting work will doubtless meet with great success. John Halifax, the hero of this most beautiful story, is no ordinary hero, and this his history is no ordinary book. It is a full-length portrait of a true gentleman, one of nature's own nobility. It is also the history of a home, and a thoroughly English one. The work abounds in incident, and is full of graphic power and true pathos. It is a book that few will read without becoming wiser and better."—*Scotsman.*

III.—THE CRESCENT AND THE CROSS.
BY ELIOT WARBURTON.

"Independent of its value as an original narrative, and its useful and interesting information, this work is remarkable for the colouring power and play of fancy with which its descriptions are enlivened. Among its greatest and most lasting charms is its reverent and serious spirit."—*Quarterly Review.*

IV.—NATHALIE. By JULIA KAVANAGH.

"'Nathalie' is Miss Kavanagh's best imaginative effort. Its manner is gracious and attractive. Its matter is good. A sentiment, a tenderness, are commanded by her which are as individual as they are elegant."—*Athenæum.*

V.—A WOMAN'S THOUGHTS ABOUT WOMEN.
BY THE AUTHOR OF "JOHN HALIFAX, GENTLEMAN."

"A book of sound counsel. It is one of the most sensible works of its kind, well-written, true-hearted, and altogether practical. Whoever wishes to give advice to a young lady may thank the author for means of doing so."—*Examiner.*

VI.—ADAM GRAEME. By MRS. OLIPHANT.

"A story awakening genuine emotions of interest and delight by its admirable pictures of Scottish life and scenery. The author sets before us the essential attributes of Christian virtue, their deep and silent workings in the heart, and their beautiful manifestations in life, with a delicacy, power, and truth which can hardly be surpassed."—*Post*

VII.—SAM SLICK'S WISE SAWS AND MODERN INSTANCES.

"The reputation of this book will stand as long as that of Scott's or Bulwer's Novels. Its remarkable originality and happy descriptions of American life still continue the subject of universal admiration. The new edition forms a part of Messrs. Hurst and Blackett's Cheap Standard Library, which has included some of the very best specimens of light literature that ever have been written."—*Messenger.*

VIII.—CARDINAL WISEMAN'S RECOLLECTIONS OF THE LAST FOUR POPES.

"A picturesque book on Rome and its ecclesiastical sovereigns, by an eloquent Roman Catholic. Cardinal Wiseman has treated a special subject with so much geniality, that his recollections will excite no ill-feeling in those who are most conscientiously opposed to every idea of human infallibility represented in Papal domination."—*Athenæum.*

IX.—A LIFE FOR A LIFE.

BY THE AUTHOR OF "JOHN HALIFAX, GENTLEMAN."

"In 'A Life for a Life' the author is fortunate in a good subject, and has produced a work of strong effect."—*Athenæum.*

X.—THE OLD COURT SUBURB. By LEIGH HUNT.

"A delightful book, that will be welcome to all readers, and most welcome to those who have a love for the best kinds of reading."—*Examiner.*

"A more agreeable and entertaining book has not been published since Boswell produced his reminiscences of Johnson."—*Observer.*

XI.—MARGARET AND HER BRIDESMAIDS.

"We recommend all who are in search of a fascinating novel to read this work for themselves. They will find it well worth their while. There are a freshness and originality about it quite charming."—*Athenæum.*

XII.—THE OLD JUDGE. By SAM SLICK.

"The publications included in this Library have all been of good quality; many give information while they entertain, and of that class the book before us is a specimen. The manner in which the Cheap Editions forming the series is produced, deserves especial mention. The paper and print are unexceptionable; there is a steel engraving in each volume, and the outsides of them will satisfy the purchaser who likes to see books in handsome uniform."—*Examiner.*

XIII.—DARIEN. By ELIOT WARBURTON.

"This last production of the author of 'The Crescent and the Cross' has the same elements of a very wide popularity. It will please its thousands."—*Globe.*

XIV.—FAMILY ROMANCE; OR, DOMESTIC ANNALS OF THE ARISTOCRACY.

BY SIR BERNARD BURKE, ULSTER KING OF ARMS.

"It were impossible to praise too highly this most interesting book. It ought to be found on every drawing-room table."—*Standard.*

XV.—THE LAIRD OF NORLAW. By MRS. OLIPHANT.

"The 'Laird of Norlaw' fully sustains the author's high reputation."—*Sunday Times.*

XVI.—THE ENGLISHWOMAN IN ITALY.

"We can praise Mrs. Gretton's book as interesting, unexaggerated, and full of opportune instruction."—*Times.*

XVII.—NOTHING NEW.

BY THE AUTHOR OF "JOHN HALIFAX, GENTLEMAN."

"'Nothing New' displays all those superior merits which have made 'John Halifax' one of the most popular works of the day."—*Post.*

XVIII.—FREER'S LIFE OF JEANNE D'ALBRET.

"Nothing can be more interesting than Miss Freer's story of the life of Jeanne D'Albret, and the narrative is as trustworthy as it is attractive."—*Post.*

XIX.—THE VALLEY OF A HUNDRED FIRES.

BY THE AUTHOR OF "MARGARET AND HER BRIDESMAIDS."

"If asked to classify this work, we should give it a place between 'John Halifax' and The Caxtons.'"—*Standard.*

XX.—THE ROMANCE OF THE FORUM.

BY PETER BURKE, SERGEANT AT LAW.

"A work of singular interest, which can never fail to charm. The present cheap and elegant edition includes the true story of the Colleen Bawn."—*Illustrated News.*

XXI.—ADELE. By JULIA KAVANAGH.

"'Adele' is the best work we have read by Miss Kavanagh; it is a charming story, full of delicate character-painting."—*Athenæum.*

XXII.—STUDIES FROM LIFE.

BY THE AUTHOR OF "JOHN HALIFAX, GENTLEMAN."

"These 'Studies from Life' are remarkable for graphic power and observation. The book will not diminish the reputation of the accomplished author."—*Saturday Review.*

XXIII.—GRANDMOTHER'S MONEY.

"We commend 'Grandmother's Money' to readers in search of a good novel. The characters are true to human nature, the story is interesting."—*Athenæum.*

XXIV.—A BOOK ABOUT DOCTORS.

BY J. C. JEAFFRESON.

"A delightful book."—*Athenæum.* "A book to be read and re-read; fit for the study as well as the drawing-room table and the circulating library."—*Lancet.*

XXV.—NO CHURCH.

"We advise all who have the opportunity to read this book."—*Athenæum.*

XXVI.—MISTRESS AND MAID.

BY THE AUTHOR OF "JOHN HALIFAX, GENTLEMAN."

"A good wholesome book, gracefully written, and as pleasant to read as it is instructive."—*Athenæum.* "A charming tale charmingly told."—*Standard.*

XXVII.—LOST AND SAVED. By HON. MRS. NORTON.

"'Lost and Saved' will be read with eager interest. It is a vigorous novel."—*Times.*
"A novel of rare excellence. It is Mrs. Norton's best prose work."—*Examiner.*

XXVIII.—LES MISERABLES. By VICTOR HUGO.

AUTHORISED COPYRIGHT ENGLISH TRANSLATION.

"The merits of 'Les Miserables' do not merely consist in the conception of it as a whole; it abounds, page after page, with details of unequalled beauty. In dealing with all the emotions, doubts, fears, which go to make up our common humanity, M. Victor Hugo has stamped upon every page the hall-mark of genius."—*Quarterly Review.*

XXIX.—BARBARA'S HISTORY.

BY AMELIA B. EDWARDS.

"It is not often that we light upon a novel of so much merit and interest as 'Barbara's History.' It is a work conspicuous for taste and literary culture. It is a very graceful and charming book, with a well-managed story, clearly-cut characters, and sentiments expressed with an exquisite elocution. It is a book which the world will like. This is high praise of a work of art, and so we intend it."—*Times.*

XXX.—LIFE OF THE REV. EDWARD IRVING.

BY MRS. OLIPHANT.

"A good book on a most interesting theme."—*Times.*
"A truly interesting and most affecting memoir. Irving's Life ought to have a niche in every gallery of religious biography. There are few lives that will be fuller of instruction, interest, and consolation."—*Saturday Review.*
"Mrs. Oliphant's Life of Irving supplies a long-felt desideratum. It is copious earnest and eloquent."—*Edinburgh Review.*

XXXI.—ST. OLAVE'S.

"This charming novel is the work of one who possesses a great talent for writing, as well as experience and knowledge of the world. 'St. Olave's' is the work of an artist. The whole book is worth reading."—*Athenæum.*

XXXII.—SAM SLICK'S AMERICAN HUMOUR.

" Dip where you will into this lottery of fun, you are sure to draw out a prize."—*Post.*

XXXIII.—CHRISTIAN'S MISTAKE.

BY THE AUTHOR OF " JOHN HALIFAX, GENTLEMAN."

" A more charming story, to our taste, has rarely been written. The writer has hit off a circle of varied characters all true to nature. Even if tried by the standard of the Archbishop of York, we should expect that even he would pronounce 'Christian's Mistake' a novel without a fault."—*Times.*

XXXIV.—ALEC FORBES OF HOWGLEN.

BY GEORGE MAC DONALD, LL.D.

" No account of this story would give any idea of the profound interest that pervades the work from the first page to the last."—*Athenæum.*

XXXV.—AGNES. By MRS. OLIPHANT.

" 'Agnes' is a novel superior to any of Mrs. Oliphant's former works."—*Athenæum.*
" A story whose pathetic beauty will appeal irresistibly to all readers."—*Post.*

XXXVI.—A NOBLE LIFE.

BY THE AUTHOR OF " JOHN HALIFAX, GENTLEMAN."

" This is one of those pleasant tales in which the author of 'John Halifax' speaks out of a generous heart the purest truths of life."—*Examiner.*

XXXVII.—NEW AMERICA. By HEPWORTH DIXON.

" A very interesting book. Mr. Dixon has written thoughtfully and well."—*Times.*
Mr. Dixon's very entertaining and instructive work on New America."—*Pall Mall Gaz.*
" We recommend every one who feels any interest in human nature to read Mr. Dixon's very interesting book."—*Saturday Review.*

XXXVIII.—ROBERT FALCONER.

BY GEORGE MAC DONALD, LL.D.

" 'Robert Falconer' is a work brimful of life and humour and of the deepest human interest. It is a book to be returned to again and again for the deep and searching knowledge it evinces of human thoughts and feelings."—*Athenæum.*

XXXIX.—THE WOMAN'S KINGDOM.

BY THE AUTHOR OF " JOHN HALIFAX, GENTLEMAN."

" 'The Woman's Kingdom' sustains the author's reputation as a writer of the purest and noblest kind of domestic stories.—*Athenæum.*

XL.—ANNALS OF AN EVENTFUL LIFE.

BY GEORGE WEBBE DASENT, D.C.L.

" A racy, well-written, and original novel. The interest never flags. The whole work sparkles with wit and humour."—*Quarterly Review.*

XLI.—DAVID ELGINBROD.

BY GEORGE MAC DONALD, LL.D.

" A novel which is the work of a man of true genius. It will attract the highest class of readers."—*Times.*

XLII.—A BRAVE LADY.

BY THE AUTHOR OF " JOHN HALIFAX, GENTLEMAN."

" A very good novel; a thoughtful, well-written book, showing a tender sympathy with human nature, and permeated by a pure and noble spirit."—*Examiner.*

XLIII.—HANNAH.

BY THE AUTHOR OF " JOHN HALIFAX, GENTLEMAN."

" A powerful novel of social and domestic life. One of the most successful efforts of a successful novelist."—*Daily News.*
" A very pleasant, healthy story, well and artistically told. The book is sure of a wide circle of readers. The character of Hannah is one of rare beauty."—*Standard*